THE SHAKESPEARE CONSPIRACY

A Novel

by

Jeffrey Hunter McQuain

TELEMACHUS PRESS

Cover designed by Telemachus Press, LLC

Cover art:
Copyright © iStockphoto/852130_DNY59
Copyright © iStockphoto/49023568_The Palmer

Published by Telemachus Press, LLC
http://www.telemachuspress.com

Visit the author website:
http://www.btglobe.com

ISBN: 978-1-941536-78-0 (eBook)
ISBN: 978-1-941536-79-7 (Paperback)

Version 2014.12.11

Printed in the United States of America

10 9 8 7 6 5 4 3 2 1

For Dan Stephen McQuain

"Wilt thou conceal this dark conspiracy?"
—William Shakespeare, "Richard II"

THE SHAKESPEARE CONSPIRACY

A Novel

THE FIRST ACT:
COLD BLOOD

Prologue

"WHO'S THERE?"

The words boomed ominously through an oaken door behind the Rose Theater and echoed along the darkened alley beyond, scattering into a windswept night along the south bank of the Thames. Outside the Rose, a sea captain and a lanky youth stood shivering against the blasts of piercing winds that failed to dissipate a permeating stench of sewage and dead fish.

"No names," the old man gruffly admonished his inquisitor within. Slowly the thick door swung open, revealing a shadowy room within. The two visitors squinted anxiously at the small gathering of men about a rounded table. At the center of the table, a candle flickered wildly, its base nestled inside a human skull.

The new arrivals staggered inside. The old man, glassy-eyed and unsteady, leant heavily on the youth, almost causing both of them to stumble.

"We were beginning to worry," the leader of the group announced as he led the older man into the dusky interior of the Rose. The boy, rewarded with a small coin for having delivered the man safely, backed up uneasily against a timbered wall to await further instruction. "And now, my good friends," the leader turned to the half-dozen men at the table, "I present to you our most deserving captain."

His words brought an immediate hush to the secretive meeting, and all eyes turned expectantly to inspect their visitor, a stout bearded man trying awkwardly to remove the rain-dampened cloak he was wearing.

"Let us proceed," the leader announced officiously, "with the night's business. We will count hands to choose our captain here or else Bartholemew, with whom you are already acquainted. Either would make a splendid addition to our school."

He paused before the final word to proffer a wide grin, eliciting appreciative laughter. The group took turns lifting tankards of ale from the table and celebrating the task of electing a new member.

The captain's eyes shone red as he looked drunkenly around the gathering. He studied the candlelit faces of gentlemen he knew from the royal court, people of substance in whose company he had long wished to be accepted. Tonight, he reveled, would be his chance at last.

"I am most honored, sir," he volunteered to the leader and bowed. The group of celebrants catcalled and whistled their approbation.

"Our captain here is familiar to many of us already," the leader genially reminded his colleagues. "Unlike Bartholemew, he is a man of competence and ability, a worthy voyager known for bringing to our shores shiploads of strangers. Strange men from distant lands. Many, many shiploads of strangers to our English shores. I say we must now reward him for all that kindness."

Striding to the far side of the room, he cracked open a small door and gestured for the captain to enter the dark space beyond.

"If you will, good friend, please wait in here with Bartholemew for our decision. We shall not need long."

He flashed the captain a conspiratorial wink and received an inebriated grin in return. The newcomer stopped briefly before the inner door, bemused by the unlit area ahead of him, but the leader reassured him with a firm clasp of a hand on his shoulder and a gentle push. "It will not take long, sir, I assure you. Have you met Bartholemew?"

The sea captain shook his head, looking into the darkness ahead. "I was told that no names were to be spoken," he said uncertainly.

The inside door was shut tight behind him, cutting off his feeble protests along with the candlelight. Then the leader signaled others nearby to help secure the door. They turned back to the table and again hoisted the tankards that had been warming their clandestine discussions.

It was not long until the first sounds of surprise began to emerge from inside the sealed room.

"Our captain seems to have met his rival," the leader of the school observed, and a few of the older men chuckled approvingly. He waited for silence to continue. "At our next gathering," he informed those in attendance, "we shall be inviting a certain young player here in Southwark to attend."

"Who?" a voice called out eagerly, and the cry was seconded by others nearby.

"Which player is it?"

"Who is he?"

"No names," the school's leader remonstrated good-naturedly, "but this much I can promise. We all make his praise."

A raucous laugh from the group covered a series of short screams that had started to emerge from the neighboring room. The leader scratched his head, raising his voice to be heard above the din.

"I must have forgotten to tell our captain," he said, lifting a tankard to toast the revelers, "that Bartholemew is a bear."

Southwark, United Kingdom, this October

School had ended for the afternoon, and the secretary rushed to lock its front door from the inside. She sat at her desk, impatiently gnawing the bear claw she'd bought at a London bakery that morning. Then she tossed the stale pastry aside in disgust and stared at the wall clock.

Finally, her desk phone began to ring. Three rings exactly, she counted. She picked up the receiver, then immediately lowered it back onto its cradle. Again she lifted the phone, this time punching in a long series of numbers and listening. On the third ring, the call was answered, and just as abruptly the connection was cut off at the other end.

The secretary blinked her hazel eyes, satisfied that all must be going as planned. From the bottom desk drawer, she withdrew a thin wrapper marked PE-4 and placed it inside her scuffed purple handbag. Tomorrow, she thought as she smoothed her skirt, she would have time to shop for a new purse in Paris.

After another glance at the clock, she flicked off the lights and locked the door from the outside. She knew she needed to hurry to board her train at St. Pancras International. Night was coming soon.

Chapter 1.

Washington, D.C., late October

"WE ALL MAKE his praise ..."

Mason Everly, coughing up blood, could not hear the words spoken behind him. With a long blade still firmly embedded in his back, the retired scholar stumbled down the Opera House steps into the main hallway of the John F. Kennedy Center for the Performing Arts. He stopped there in the Grand Foyer, one of the world's largest rooms, and felt the killer's hand brace against him to extract the deep-thrust dagger.

Staggering forward, Everly released his grip on a briefcase, which dropped noiselessly onto the plush red carpet suffusing Kennedy Center. He lurched across the enormous hallway, awkwardly embracing the stone pedestal beneath a giant bronze bust of John Fitzgerald Kennedy's face.

The gray-haired professor of Renaissance history glanced wildly about, but there was no one near him in the 600-foot corridor of marble walls and crystal chandeliers. It was Halloween, and a drizzly October afternoon in the District of Columbia meant fewer tourists in the Center than normal.

Minutes earlier, Everly deliberately lagged behind a walking tour of the memorial. He had made his way unobserved inside the empty Opera House. When he emerged from the theater a moment later, the dagger entered his back, tearing through the flesh, and he slumped forward, dizzied with pain.

Desperate to regain his balance, Everly clung to the base of the assassinated President's sculpture. He pinched the gold stud in his left earlobe to concentrate on what needed to be done. Then he shoved himself away from the pedestal, lunging toward a set of tall glass doors leading out to a marble terrace and the Potomac River beyond.

Mere steps behind him, the hooded killer taunted him, repeating a mantra obscured by a mask. "We all ... make his praise."

Anguished by the effort, Everly inched open the nearest exit to find himself outside Kennedy Center in a steady afternoon rain. He pressed his face against the cool glass of the door as pellets of water cascaded into a shallow puddle at his feet. Realizing his left hand still clutched the London Fog coat he'd worn into Washington that morning, he knew what he had to do.

Everly carefully unfolded the coat onto the walkway. With his head spinning, he pushed wet strands of gray hair out of his eyes and knelt achingly down. His hand refused to work at first, but he reached slowly back to his wound and then outstretched his trembling fingers to mark the glass door in front of him. Then he waited.

From close by him came the gentle whisk of another door being opened, and all too soon he heard the words one last time.

"We all make his praise."

Chapter 2.

CHRISTOPHER KLEWE ANXIOUSLY paced the long hall inside Washington's Folger Shakespeare Library, his rugged young face lined with concern.

Klewe, a renowned Shakespeare professor from William and Mary, paused as he always did to gaze into the final case in the Folger's dark-timbered gallery. Beneath a surface of glass, this cabinet contained the First Folio, a 1623 copy worth more than five million dollars. The book, opened to its title page, displayed as always the apostrophe-lacking title ("Mr. William Shakespeares Comedies, Histories, and Tragedies"), as well as the engraved black-and-white portrait of the world's most famous writer. This time, though, Klewe's chance to study that engraving was short-lived.

"One down," snapped a female voice behind him. Before he could respond, a folded newspaper was backhanded onto the glass counter in front of him, obscuring his view of Shakespeare's face.

He turned to find an attractive woman in her late 20's, a tawny windbreaker draped over one arm. She skimmed off a gold-and-burgundy scarf to reveal long blond hair framing a nearly symmetrical face.

"Three letters long," she continued matter of factly, tugging at the long sleeves of her rumpled turtleneck sweater. "The clue reads 'Shakespeare insult,' and I think it starts with a D."

Removing the paper from the glass without looking at it, Klewe handed the crossword puzzle back to her. "DWM," he said.

She frowned uncertainly. "That's not a word."

"It's an abbreviation. Stands for Dead White Male."

"You mean like Dead Presidents?"

"No, that's money. DWM is an insult. It's used by someone dismissing the work of Shakespeare or any writer who happens to be a Dead White Male as irrelevant." Klewe returned to his scrutiny of the Bard's face inside the display, and she bent across his shoulder for a closer look. He appreciated the gentle scent that drifted toward him, recognizing the fragrance as Obsession.

"Is that really him?" This time when he looked up at her, she offered a warm smile. "After all, you are the rock star of Shakespeare studies, Professor Klewe."

"You know who I am?"

"Of course."

Having just turned 30, Christopher Klewe had already achieved international fame as the cutting-edge expert on Shakespeare's codes and hidden meanings, but he still found celebrity a bemusing business. He much preferred spending his time in a classroom or the library stacks than in the public spotlight.

Earlier that day, he'd driven his Jeep for three hours from Williamsburg to D.C. to do research in the Folger's underground reading room. He always enjoyed working there, situated between a reproduction of the bust from Shakespeare's tomb and a stained-glass tribute to the Seven Ages of Man speech in "As You Like It." When he finished his work, he'd come upstairs for afternoon tea but was sidetracked as usual by the Folio picture. He turned from the glass case toward the young woman in the charcoal turtleneck and dark Guess jeans as she stamped her half-boots against the floor.

"Nobody knows," he admitted, "what Shakespeare really looked like. At least not for sure." Self-consciously straightening a loosely knotted yellow tie, he sensed that his blue sports coat and khakis had probably tagged him as an English teacher.

She stared inquisitively at the Folio's familiar Martin Droeshout engraving of the Bard, with the rounded pale face, drooping mustache and extremely high hairline. "Well, this picture had better be accurate. I would hate to think how many people have been taken in by it. Wouldn't you?"

Her side of the conversation continued, but Klewe was having trouble focusing on her words. He flexed his arms in a large sweeping motion and stifled a yawn.

"Sorry," he said. "It's not the company." He motioned her to sit with him on a nearby bench. From inside his blue blazer, he produced a small Cartier pocket watch encased in silver. "I'm waiting for a colleague, but he's late." Clicking the watch shut, he placed it back in his jacket. "I was about to check my phone messages."

They were distracted by a group of tourists noisily exiting the high-paneled room of oak and plaster. Aside from empty suits of armor and a security guard at the far end, they now had the Elizabethan long hall to themselves. Klewe, not finding his phone, pulled a small pad from his pocket and scribbled a quick note about his newest project. It had the potential, he knew, of becoming the most explosive Shakespeare book of this generation. As he finished writing the note to himself, he glanced upward to find the young woman also jotting in a wire-bound notebook.

She studied his face as carefully as the Folio portrait. "Dark wavy hair," she said as she wrote. "Inscrutable brown eyes. A Johnny Depp intensity."

He watched her make another notation and then put away the notebook. Sighing, she gathered a fistful of her blond hair into a ponytail and let it drop casually across her shoulders. After opening a pack of Wrigley's Doublemint, she offered him some gum. When he declined, she began chewing a stick herself vigorously.

"I came here to see you," she announced.

Most people who sought him out wanted Klewe to inscribe his current best-seller, "The Great Shakespeare Mysteries," a book of hidden messages in the Bard's plays and poems. The young woman, however, was making no effort to produce a copy for him to sign.

"You've read my book?" he tried coaxing her.

"No, sorry. It wasn't a murder mystery." She thought for a moment. "That's what you should write."

Klewe stared back at her. "Who are you?"

"Zelda Hart." She removed a wallet from the beige Coach bag slung across her shoulder and flashed a business card in his direction. "New York Times."

"I see," he said slowly. "I'm afraid I have no time available for an interview today, Miss Hart."

"Mrs. Hart, but Zelda will do." She twisted the ring on her left hand. "And that's not what I was told, Professor. I was told to meet you here for tea this afternoon. You and your colleague."

He kept his gaze noncommittal.

"While we're waiting, though, I am stuck on another answer." She handed him back the crossword. "Nine letters, starting with C, and it's a real killer."

"I really don't have time," he began uncertainly.

"This whole puzzle's about famous writers. Let me read you the clue: 'Died in 1616 the same date but not the same day as Shakespeare.' What could that mean?"

Klewe hesitated an instant and reached for her pen. After filling in the name, he handed the puzzle back to her, and she examined it carefully.

Zelda arched an eyebrow. "Are you sure?" He nodded, and she returned the folded newspaper to her shoulder bag. "Thanks," she told him. "But what I'm really here to find out is what you're up to. At least, that's what your friend promised me in his email." She dug deeper into the open Coach bag to retrieve a crumpled paper that she then flattened out to hand him. "Here's a hard copy."

> To: Zelda Hart
> From: Mason Everly
> Re: Shakespeare's Secret
>
> Come to Folger tea today at four. Chris Klewe will reveal the biggest cover-up in literary history. You'll never view Shakespeare the same way again.

Klewe read the page repeatedly. As he read, he was trying hard not to express his dismay at its contents.

"So tell me," she finally said, bending toward him conspiratorially, "what's the deep dark secret?"

Chapter 3.

DAMN IT, KLEWE said to himself, what could Mason be thinking? The media announcement for their new book was to be made in London in a few days. Why bring in a reporter now?

He slowly refolded the page while he considered the right response for discouraging her. She indicated for him to keep the paper, which he pocketed.

"How do you know Mason?" he finally asked.

"I don't. Never met him except online." With an ebullient smile that charmed Klewe, Zelda said, "Does it have to be tea? It's good for antioxidants and all that, but how about something stronger? First round of vanilla vodka's on me."

"I'm afraid not, Mrs. Hart. I think there's been some sort of mistake made. As you can see, Professor Everly has yet to arrive, and when he does—" Suddenly they heard a minor commotion near the far end of the Folger gallery. He stopped, silently welcoming the interruption.

From beside the guard's desk, a young policeman in a crisp uniform approached, holding his hat upside down in front of him like an offering plate. He identified himself as Officer Chad Cooper with the District of Columbia Police Department, his sandy hair carefully combed and cherubic face marked only by the small nick of a razor.

"Are you Professor Christopher Klewe?" He waited for a slight nod. "Professor, there's been some trouble at Kennedy Center. A murder." He checked his notes. "Of a Professor Mason Everly."

Stunned, Klewe rose to his feet. "Mason?"

"Yes, sir. I'm sorry to tell you he was stabbed to death a few hours ago."

"My God, who would do such a thing?"

The youthful officer hesitated. "We don't know yet. Detective Edmund Robinson from D.C. Homicide asked me to bring you to Kennedy Center for a few questions. My car's outside, if you could come along with me."

A distraught Klewe followed him from the long hall and grabbed his umbrella at a stand inside the main entrance. Behind them, Zelda scrambled to gather her wet belongings and keep pace.

"I'm sorry, ma'am, just Professor Klewe," Officer Cooper was telling Zelda, but she edged past the policeman to grab Klewe's arm.

"I work for him," Zelda proclaimed defiantly. Klewe, his mind whirling about his colleague's death, was vaguely surprised but said nothing to contradict her.

They passed through the Folger reception area, with the guard's desk on one side and a small gift shop on the other. Inside the gift shop was a wall decorated with latex Halloween masks of Shakespeare's face, surrounded by assorted hand puppets and action figures of the Bard. Adjacent displays featured various editions of Shakespeare's works as well as copies of Klewe's latest book. He stopped short, looking puzzled.

"Are you all right?" Zelda asked.

Klewe forced a weak smile. "It's funny, but I never come into this building without thinking of Abby Folger. She was an heiress to the Folger's Coffee fortune and related to the family who built the library."

"What about her?"

"She was murdered too. One of Charles Manson's victims."

Klewe said nothing more. Zelda hastened to retie her scarf while the police officer motioned him aside.

"I'm sorry about your colleague, but Detective Robinson did want me to ask you something. The attack didn't seem to be a robbery. Your friend had identification on him, and they didn't take his wallet or his watch."

"So?"

Cooper deliberately turned away from Zelda and asked quietly, "So why would they have taken his ear?"

Without answering, Klewe pushed past him to get some air. He waited outside, studying the front of the Folger building with its Art Deco design and its masks of comedy and tragedy over the doors. Across the library's exterior were white bas-reliefs of scenes from Shakespeare's plays, and his eyes locked on the carving for "Julius Caesar." It showed Caesar's stabbing death by conspirators, and Klewe wondered mournfully what his friend's last moments must have been like. Then he heard Zelda call him over to the opened door of an unmarked police car.

Once they struggled inside, Officer Cooper maneuvered the gray Crown Victoria onto East Capitol Street and drove away from the Folger, Zelda and Klewe silent in the back seat. Nobody spoke as they passed the tall marble columns of the Supreme Court building or the majestic dome of the U.S. Capitol. After Cooper turned off Pennsylvania Avenue, though, Zelda edged forward to glimpse a stately neoclassical facade ahead.

"You're the Einstein," she said to Klewe. "What's that?"

He followed the direction of her index finger.

"The National Archives," he answered flatly. In no mood to converse, he tried pretending to enjoy the reds and bronzes of the changing leaves around them. The afternoon rain had let up, and the District felt unseasonably warm for the end of October.

"I know that much," she responded. "Home of the Declaration of Independence and about four million other documents. I meant, what's that written outside?"

Before them towered the marble statue of a female figure representing the future, and engraved in her stone pedestal was a brief quotation:

WHAT IS PAST
IS PROLOGUE.

Klewe sat up to view the inscription and then drew back. "That's Shakespeare. Well, sort of. It misquotes 'The Tempest.'" She gave him a quizzical look. "It should have said, 'What's past is prologue.' It's not all that unusual, though. This whole town is plastered with everything from Shakespearean quotes to Freemason symbols. Look around Washington sometime, and you'll be surprised what all's hidden in plain sight."

Zelda read the engraved quotation again carefully. "But what is it supposed to mean?"

"The quote? It means everything that's gone before— whatever has happened up until this very moment—is only an introduction for what's ahead. In other words, you can't change the past, so you'd better get ready for what's coming."

As the car moved on, he glanced back at the inscription on the statue. "What is past is prologue," he read again. And then, in spite of himself, he shuddered.

Chapter 4.

AFTER A QUICK drive through Northwest Washington, they could spot the exterior of Kennedy Center shimmering ahead of them. In the half-light of the overcast afternoon, the Center's giant cakebox design showed off gleaming white marble supported by columns of gold. The three of them climbed out of the Ford four-door against a short hill, and Officer Cooper led them around the east side of the massive building, taking cautious steps on the rain-slick surface of its long white promenade.

Nearing the Potomac River side of the Center, Klewe deliberately slowed his steps further and began taking a series of deep breaths. The three of them had to weave through a swarm of police and security officers along the memorial until they reached the terrace in back. There they found strands of luminescent yellow tape marking off an area beside tall glass doors.

Klewe halted, hoping the body of his friend had been removed from the crime scene, but there were too many people around to be certain. He and Zelda surveyed a multitude of officials trading curt questions and one-word answers. Cooper stepped aside to confer with another uniformed officer near the tape and then came striding back, motioning them toward the riverside railing.

"Who are all these people?" Zelda asked.

The officer started counting on his fingers. "Let's see. There's D.C.P.D., of course. Also, the Park Police who oversee Washington's memorials, the F.B.I., C.I.A., Homeland Security, Secret Service. It's a national monument, so everybody's trying to grab turf, and somewhere in this crowd I'm supposed to locate Detective Robinson. I'll be right back."

"No problem," Zelda said as he walked away. When she turned to see the ashen face on Klewe, she realized she'd spoken too soon, but the officer was already gone. "Sorry. I wasn't thinking. You shouldn't be out here where it happened."

"It's not just that." He turned his back to the railing and took a half-seated position on a marble ledge. "It's that." He jerked a thumb over his shoulder.

"Roosevelt Island?" She studied the dark land mass in the middle of the Potomac. Now a natural preserve, the elongated island overgrown with trees was named for the outdoorsman Theodore Roosevelt and had become a magnet for District ornithologists. From dusk onward, the bird sanctuary remained dark, sporting none of the intrusive lights that illuminate most of Washington in the evening.

"No. I meant the Potomac." Klewe turned to Zelda. "I have this thing."

"What thing?"

"About rivers."

He noticed her skeptical look. "It sounds silly, but I've had it ever since I was little. When I was five, my family went camping along the James River in Virginia, and my brother Jackson pushed me headfirst into a deep spot. I was swept half a mile downstream before they found me."

Zelda gave him a sympathetic stare.

"The worst feeling of my entire life," he continued, "all that water swirling above my head, and then I was on the bank, coming to and gasping for breath. I thought I was going to die, and ever since then—well, they tell me I'm not the only one who has a fear of moving water. It's called potamophobia, a word I really hate. Whenever I'm near a river, I tell myself it's all in my mind, but …"

"Then let's move." She took his arm reassuringly and tugged him a few steps away from the Potomac overlook. "Don't worry about it. Everybody has something that bothers them."

"Really? What bothers a New York Times reporter?"

"Spiders," she said decisively. "Can't stand them. Did you know CNN took a poll once and found out it's the single biggest fear of Americans?" Zelda hesitated. "But I shouldn't be doing the talking. I'm not the one being interviewed."

"Neither am I," he reminded her.

"We'll see."

Officer Cooper came back across the terrace to them. "I need you to wait here a little while longer."

"No can do," Zelda announced in a voice loud enough for every last one of the surrounding officials to glare at them. "This man has a fear of rivers, so I'm taking him inside right now." She gave Klewe an impish smile. As she led him away, she whispered to him, "Sorry. Couldn't resist."

"Of course not," he replied dryly.

The light from inside Kennedy Center played across Klewe's bright red face as he trudged along beside her into the building. He and Zelda stopped just inside the nearest door and, like millions of tourists before them, ogled the stunning display of the Grand Foyer, its tremendous length garnished with shiny Italian marble and plush red carpeting. Overhead was a dazzling array of imported crystal chandeliers, and not far away was the enormous sculptured face of Kennedy himself, raised eight feet off the floor. Set on a stone pedestal, it was positioned near the Opera House, midway between the Eisenhower Theater and the Concert Hall. At the distant end of the corridor stood the Millennium Stage, an open platform for free musical and dramatic performances.

Nobody was performing at the moment, however, and Klewe kept staring at Kennedy's giant face of bronze. What was it, he thought to himself as he searched his memory, Mason Everly had said about the Center's metallic art? He recalled the answer silently with a satisfied smile.

Officer Cooper came back into view, and they watched him outside the glass doors as he was being given photographs by crime-scene workers.

"Sorry I embarrassed you," Zelda repeated. Klewe had the feeling he was being set up again, but she opened her shoulder bag and reached in to remove a small rounded object. No bigger than an inch across, the ornament's glass cover encased tiny greenish leaves. "Here's a gift that should make you feel better."

"What is it?" he asked suspiciously.

"A four-leaf clover, picked from the grave of William Shakespeare himself. I hear it brings you good luck." She slipped the keepsake into his blazer pocket. "Thought maybe you could use it."

"Thanks," he responded without enthusiasm. "I feel much better."

The officer approached them with two photos in hand. The first showed a dagger, its blade almost eight inches long and the grip covered with twisted wire, its pommel perfectly rounded.

"Detective Robinson said to show you this weapon. We got the image off Kennedy Center's security cameras and enlarged it."

"That's called a main-gauche," Klewe said, studying the design. "It's French for 'left hand.' When a swordfighter wields the rapier in his right hand, he can use a dagger like that in his left to parry thrusts and inflict more damage on his opponent. This one looks like it could be more than 400 years old."

"I'll let the detective know," Cooper said before revealing the second photograph. "He also wanted me to show you this." It depicted a large glass door with the letters "SoN" smeared across the surface. "Do those letters mean anything to you, Professor?"

Klewe studied the scrawled characters without recognition. "Should they?"

"The picture was taken outside these doors, next to where we found your colleague."

"It looks like 'son' to me," Klewe said, "but Mason didn't have children."

"Maybe he was spelling out part of his name." Zelda moved closer to examine the lettering. "What is that written with?"

"Blood," Cooper answered.

They were silent for a moment.

Zelda, fixated on the picture, asked, "You think he wrote that himself?" When the police officer nodded, she looked outside to where crime-scene workers continued their painstaking collection of evidence. "Was anything else found?"

"They're not done yet." Cooper walked them away from the glass doors. "But we did find one thing unusual. His raincoat."

"That's not so unusual," Klewe said. "It's a rainy day."

"Not the coat itself. It's the way we found it. Laid out evenly on the wet ground for him to kneel down on. Most people when they're dying don't care whether their pants get wet. They'll let go of whatever they're holding, and then later on we find belongings from the victim scattered everywhere. But this time we have a raincoat stretched out carefully on the ground. What do you make of that?"

Neither Klewe nor Zelda had a response.

Cooper checked his wristwatch. "The detective should be ready by now. This way."

"I suppose I'm to wait here?" Zelda asked Klewe.

"If you like," he said, feigning special attention to the rough-hewn surface of the Kennedy bust. "You know, Mason once told me about some metallic art here that was starting to discolor. They were afraid the metal was turning white with age."

"I don't see anything wrong now." Zelda inspected the bronze. "Did they have it refinished?"

"Didn't need to. Turns out all the art needed was a good cleaning. Problem wasn't age after all."

"Really? What caused it?"

Officer Cooper was beckoning them to follow. Klewe, starting across the Grand Foyer, called out the reply to her question over his shoulder.

"Spiders."

Chapter 5.

SEVERAL STEPS BEFORE reaching the Concert Hall, Kennedy Center's acoustically perfect space for symphony orchestras and pop stars, Zelda had overtaken him and punched his arm playfully. "Very funny, Professor."

"Couldn't resist," he parroted her gently.

"So what do you have against reporters?"

He offered no answer as they followed Cooper upstairs to a closed set of doors. When the officer pushed wide the entrance, Klewe had been expecting to find a small nondescript office for the police interview. He couldn't believe how wrong he was.

Before their astonished eyes appeared a room that housed a Hitchcock film gone awry. Birds, and more birds, of every color, size and wingspan filled the cabinets in an elegant room lined with figurines and delicate paintings. From hummingbirds to bald eagles, the winged display seemed unnervingly alive, ready to perch upon intruders and deliver a well-deserved pecking to everybody within reach.

"Missed this room on my tour," Klewe murmured to Zelda, who was enthralled by the excess of nature about her. The collection was designed as a tribute to George Rogers Clark, the early American naturalist who never gained the renown of his younger brother William, the latter half of Lewis and Clark. Even though the room carried an official designation of the Clark Room, visitors rarely called it that.

"This," Cooper proclaimed from the entrance, "is the bird room. It's a space usually reserved for private gatherings of 60 or more, and I hear it can rent for about a thousand dollars an hour. Detective Robinson will be right in, so have a seat. But please don't break anything." He snatched away the umbrella Klewe had almost forgotten he was still carrying. "I'd better hold that for you outside."

Once the officer departed, neither Klewe nor Zelda said anything, twisting about with disbelieving eyes to observe the wildlife around them. On a normal day, Klewe would have found these representations of animal and plant life charming, but this day was anything but normal. For a moment Klewe could almost swear he heard something feeding, but the chewing turned out to be Zelda's as she indulged in a new stick of gum. She shivered and drew her windbreaker tighter, glancing to her left at the fierce expression of a looming blue jay.

As if on cue, the bird room's door burst open. Framed in the entranceway was a tall African American man with a scowling face and commanding presence. Dressed in a somber tan suit, he stopped to run a hand over his balding head and stood assessing the two of them. Almost two decades with District Homicide served to reinforce the exact impression he sought to give, that of a hawk preparing to rush its prey.

Detective Edmund Robinson came forward and introduced himself. Without shaking hands, he pulled a notebook from his pocket and took a seat facing them.

"You must be Christopher Klewe," he read from his notes, "a college professor?"

Klewe nodded. "At William and Mary. I teach Shakespeare courses there."

"That's it, that's where I know you from. You're the Shakespeare detective from Virginia. The F.B.I. called you in last year to help break that serial-killer case. The one where they found the Shakespeare clues at each body dump."

"I wasn't that much help."

Robinson reacted with surprise. "Not from what I hear. In fact, what was it the media started calling you?" Klewe knew what was coming and cringed. "Oh, yeah, now I remember. The Shakespeare Sherlock, wasn't it?"

Zelda erupted with a throaty laugh. "Oh, I get it. Klewe and all that."

"Now you know," Klewe whispered sharply to her, "what I have against reporters." He motioned toward Zelda, saying, "And this is Mrs. Hart."

"Zelda Hart," she told the detective. "I'm working with the Professor." Klewe gave her a pointed stare but did not correct her, and the detective made a quick notation on his pad.

"In fact," Robinson continued, "you were supposed to have a meeting today with Mason Everly, who was also a professor, I believe?"

"Emeritus," Klewe corrected. "He was my mentor when I went to James Madison University. I still can't believe this happened to him."

"Your friend decided to stop at Kennedy Center on his way to see you this afternoon."

"But that's just it. He wasn't even supposed to be in the country this week. He was supposed to be in London, where I'd be meeting him in a few days to give a lecture announcing our new book. So what was he doing here?"

Robinson considered the words carefully. "Had he called you from London?"

"Yes, a few days ago. Said he'd found something important."

"Any idea what that something was?"

Klewe shook his head, and the detective's scowl deepened.

"Look, Professor, I have a stabbing here at the second most popular tourist site in Washington. Everyone from the mayor to the F.B.I. director is demanding to know what happened, and all we have is a crime scene with what I'm told is a 400-year-old murder weapon. If there's anything else you can tell me, I need it now."

"Wait," Zelda said, turning to Klewe. "You never got to check your messages at the Folger, did you?"

"No," he admitted. "I keep this thing turned off when I'm doing research." He fished a BlackBerry from his coat pocket and pressed a button to light up the cell phone. "No new calls, but there is a text message. It came from Mason at 1:30 this afternoon. Now that's odd." His brow wrinkled at the short message, and he turned the phone so Robinson and Zelda could each read the two lines on its small screen.

Re: N35
"my bones"

Then he watched them both scribbling the text into their notebooks.

"That's the whole message?" Robinson asked in frustration. "What the hell does it mean?"

Klewe shrugged. "Your guess is as good as mine."

"Maybe he knew he was going to die," Zelda suggested. "You know how some people say they can feel things in their bones?"

The detective seemed unimpressed and looked at Klewe. "What about N35? Does that mean anything to you?"

"No. Perhaps it's a page reference? Or an apartment number?"

Zelda added, "Or a bingo space."

"If that text was sent to you at 1:30, it would have been close to the time of death. We've established that from security tapes."

Klewe's eyes lifted hopefully. "Could you see who did it?"

"No, it was a blitz attack. Some guy with a hood obscuring his face. The initial stabbing took place near the Opera House entrance, and the killer followed him outside to slice off the lobe of his left ear."

Zelda flinched at the macabre detail, but it made Klewe wonder. "Mason did have a small earring, a gold stud in his left ear, but I doubt it was very expensive. If robbery wasn't the motive, though, why take that?"

The detective shrugged, then consulted his notes again. "The tapes also showed Everly placing his coat on the ground to kneel down and write three letters in blood on the door." Robinson pulled out an enhanced copy of the crime-scene photo Cooper had shown them earlier. This version clearly displayed the overcoat on the watery terrace as well as "SoN" smeared in blood onto the glass. "Remarkable that somebody being murdered would spread out his coat on the ground so evenly. Would you say your colleague was excessively neat? Compulsive, maybe?"

"Never to that extreme. And I've known him for many years."

"What about the letters he wrote on the door?" the detective said. "It looks like 'son' to me, but you told Cooper he didn't have children."

"That's right."

"Maybe he meant something else," Robinson considered. "Is your new book on Shakespeare's poetry? Could be the start of 'sonnet.'"

"Or the end of 'Robinson,'" Zelda offered less than helpfully. A menacing glance from the detective made her add a hasty "sir."

Klewe turned the print from side to side. At last he commented, "The 'o' looks different. It's smaller. The others are capital letters."

"Meaning?"

"An abbreviation, maybe. They use 'So' on maps to indicate south, don't they?"

"Does 'South N' make sense to either of you?"

Neither answered immediately. Then Zelda frowned and asked, "Could that N be connected to the N35 business?"

Without responding to her, Robinson made another notation. "I have just a few more questions for you," he said, raising his eyes from the notebook. When Klewe started to speak, the detective indicated Zelda. "No, I mean you. Are you a teacher too?"

"No, she isn't," Klewe volunteered quickly to forestall another lie to the police.

"I didn't think so. So who are you?"

"A reporter," she admitted slowly. From the wallet in her bag, she produced a business card. "But I didn't think a press badge would get me in here."

"It wouldn't." The detective shot them both an angry look.

"I don't really see," Klewe began, trying hard to change the subject, "what this has to do with Mason's death."

"And I don't find either one of you very forthcoming. You say this man was a friend of yours, and yet you haven't been able to give me a single reason somebody would want him dead. The victim sends a mysterious text about bones and writes messages in his own blood, but it's meaningless to you. Is that what you expect me to believe?"

"Look," Klewe replied, "if I could be more helpful, I would. Mason was a good friend as well as a colleague. And I'm sorry about Mrs. Hart's little deception. She's only here because she was invited to meet with Mason and me this afternoon."

Zelda chewed the gum faster. "Professor Everly did send me an email to come to the Folger today, but you have to believe us. We honestly have no idea who killed him or why."

"That's not true," Klewe interrupted to finesse her statement. "In fact, I can tell you exactly why he was killed."

Surprised, they both turned to him.

"Mason Everly was helping me with some research, Detective."

"Research doesn't usually get somebody murdered."

"It can if you look into something that's controversial enough. We've been trying to prove a theory. A conspiracy theory about William Shakespeare. Something that has been covered up for four centuries now, and there are people who may not want it to be uncovered. It's a secret, maybe the biggest secret in the history of literature."

"Really?" Robinson said. "And just what secret are you hoping to reveal?"

"Yes," Zelda wondered aloud, "what kind of secret is worth dying for?"

Klewe lowered his voice, as if to keep the surrounding birds from eavesdropping on his response. "That Shakespeare was black."

Chapter 6.

ZELDA'S GUM STOPPED in mid-chew. Robinson's jaw lowered slightly, and he sat back against his chair for the first time since the interview started, wordlessly dropping his pen onto the notebook in his lap.

Nobody said anything for the longest moment. Then Klewe found himself barraged by questions from both sides of the interrogation.

"Shakespeare was black?" the detective repeated. "Are you serious?"

"How can you say that?" Zelda asked. "We all know what Shakespeare looked like. Aren't there pictures of him all over the place? We just saw one at the Folger."

"Yes, there are several pictures," Klewe acknowledged. "The problem is that no two of them look very much alike. They're just vague notions of some white male in Renaissance outfits. And more often than not those pictures were painted by people who never set eyes on Shakespeare. Nobody can say for sure what the world's greatest writer looked like, at least not from pictures drawn during his lifetime by anybody who knew him. That's what Mason was in London researching this week."

He briefly glanced at a porcelain owl hovering in the shadows of the bird room and then turned his attention back to his spellbound listeners.

"Mason had gone to the National Portrait Gallery in London last week to complete some notes for our book. I'd taken this week off to work here at the Folger and then join him in London, where he was giving a lecture to break the news of our theory at the Globe Theater. We weren't sure what to expect, though, or how the academic community might react to a radically new image of Shakespeare."

"I'm tempted," the detective said in measured syllables, "to ask if you're on drugs." Robinson repeatedly shook his head, trying to clear it. "I was sure you were going to tell me somebody else wrote Shakespeare's plays. That's what my son Kenneth was complaining about the other day. He's in high school, and his drama teacher made him memorize a sonnet, the one about comparing thee to a summer's day. Kenneth finally learned it, but he kept saying nobody even knows who wrote this stuff."

Klewe gave a tight smile. "That's the usual line, isn't it? That Shakespeare couldn't have written Shakespeare. There have been dozens and dozens of books published on the real identity of Shakespeare, as well as entire books on what his face looked like. But we simply don't know what he looked like, and I think that may have been deliberate. Part of a conspiracy to cover up the truth."

He stopped to consider his next words carefully.

"I can't tell you who killed him, Detective Robinson, but I do think that's why he's dead. Mason may have sensed something was about to happen, because he had called in the media without telling me. He invited Zelda to come see us this afternoon at the Folger." He reached into his shirt pocket and unfolded the page Zelda had given him. Robinson read over it and handed it back.

"You realize what you're saying about your friend's death?"

He nodded solemnly. "We expected there might be a backlash from our study, but nothing like this. You can't help it when you advance such a confrontational theory. Some people aren't going to like the image of a biracial Shakespeare very much."

The detective agreed. "You would be pushing the hot buttons for a lot of racists, I imagine."

"When I first approached Mason about helping me, we discussed the possible dangers, but he assured me he could handle himself. He never took the threat very seriously, it seemed to me …" His words trailed off.

"Hold on a minute," Zelda finally said, vying to become the voice of reason in what seemed a most unreasonable room. "What about Shakespeare's grave? Can't they just exhume his body and find the answer?"

"I don't think the British people would allow it," Klewe told her. "In fact, Shakespeare himself said no. At least, we think he did, if the words of his epitaph are his own. He placed a curse on anybody who dared disturb his resting place. And, as far as we know, the tomb has never been opened."

"As far as we know?" she asked him.

"Back in 1989, there was a group in the United Kingdom from Yorkshire TV, working on a documentary about Shakespeare. They were granted special permission to X-ray his tomb to see what it contained."

"And?"

"Nothing."

"Just the skeleton, you mean."

"Not even that. They said nothing showed up on the X-ray."

"Hardly surprising," Robinson declared. "When you consider that grave robbers and souvenir seekers have had hundreds of years to do their worst."

Zelda pondered a moment. "Would a skeleton have been enough for you to tell anyway? About somebody's racial identity?"

"I was told it might be," Klewe said.

The detective nodded. "Forensic anthropologists can determine a lot from human remains. For instance, scientists can tell the age of children by the development of certain bones. In adult skeletons, it's often possible to determine the sex of the person too, but that's harder to tell in children who've died before puberty."

"Is racial identification possible?"

"Well," Robinson explained, "race is not such a clearly defined matter. But I'm told experts can recognize differences between the skulls of, say, black people and white people. Of course, you'd need to have the skull to begin with."

"And there isn't one," Zelda concluded. "I imagine it's not worth asking if there are any relatives still around."

Klewe exhaled slowly. "No direct ones, at least in the known line. Not since his granddaughter died in the 17th century."

"So much for DNA," she said.

"I realize it may sound preposterous at first," Klewe told them, "but it makes sense in a lot of ways when you consider the evidence we do have. There have been rumors in theatrical circles about this for a very long time, maybe stretching all the way back to Shakespeare's time. Then a few decades ago a professor from New York University published the notion that there might have been a black person in Shakespeare's theater company. I'm just taking the speculation a step further and asking if that black person could have been Shakespeare himself."

Zelda and Robinson looked at each other in amazement.

Klewe cleared his throat. "I've been skeptical too, and I'm not even saying we can ever prove it. We have very limited information on record about Shakespeare's parents, and he didn't exactly leave us an autobiography. I'm not saying we believe it, but there are so many questions that need to be answered."

The detective picked up his notebook from his lap. "I don't know if you're expecting me to take you seriously or not. Let me wrap my head around this. You are telling me that I have a Caucasian victim in D.C. who may have been killed for suggesting that Shakespeare was black." His groan practically filled the bird room. "I have a murder that needs to be solved fast, and we don't even know whether your—how do I put this?—theory is involved. You two are free to go. For now. But I may need you again." Robinson produced a card with his contact numbers. After a short pause, his voice softened. "Good luck, Professor, but be careful."

"Can you tell me, Detective, if Mason was carrying a flash drive on him? Or maybe you found his laptop?"

Robinson rechecked his notes. "We know from the security tapes that he dropped his briefcase, and the killer retrieved it. There was no flash drive that I'm aware of."

"They aren't very big," Zelda noted, measuring an invisible one with her fingers.

"Yeah, I know what they look like. The guy didn't have one. He was carrying," Robinson ticked off a list from his notes, "a set of keys, a wallet, and a passport. He'd also scribbled a reminder to meet you at the Folger this afternoon. That's how I knew where to send Officer Cooper." He shut the notebook. "No flash drive."

A loud knock at the door summoned the detective to leave quickly for his next interview. "Don't go far," Robinson said as he flew to the door. "And watch out. If you're right about all this, you could be—" his final word echoed back toward them as he departed—"next."

Chapter 7.

ZELDA WAS INSTANTLY on her feet, whirling giddily with excitement until she nearly collided with a bobwhite. She rushed at Klewe with open arms and squeezed him about the neck. "Dance with me," she invited him.

"There's no music, and I can't dance. Why are you so happy?"

"I knew it. I just knew there was a big story here. There's been Internet buzz about some kind of Shakespeare news coming out, and I hoped there was something to it, but I never dreamed it was this big."

"Oh, great. Mason was discussing it on the Web too." Klewe's expression grew sober. "That may be how the wrong people learned about it. What had he written?"

Zelda was, however, too busy dancing to respond. She waltzed away from a precariously positioned thrush and, taking hold of Klewe's arm, led him outside the bird room. They found their way back to the Concert Hall's entrance and into the Grand Foyer near the Kennedy bust. "I can almost see it now," she predicted to him effusively.

"See what?"

"The cover of Time magazine, of course."

"Oh, of course."

"Can't you see it too? A picture of Shakespeare, his face half covered in shadow, along with a headline in big letters asking, 'Was Shakespeare Black?'"

She stopped in mid twirl and tightened her grip on Klewe.

"You do plan to let me break this story, don't you?"

"I don't know," he said tersely, and her smile faded away. They left the Grand Foyer and headed toward the Center's front doors. "What have you seen on the Internet?" he asked Zelda as they walked outside.

"Not much. Something about one of Shakespeare's poems." She flipped through her notebook to check. "Sonnet 55. Does that mean anything to your theory?"

"Everything," he answered, more dispirited than annoyed.

They crossed over the entrance plaza to the east lawn and noted a lone figure standing next to an unusual horseback sculpture. The man was flicking ashes from the end of a short cigarette and occasionally tossing a hot-tempered glance over his shoulder at the diminishing number of police and Center officials. They might have ignored the older man entirely, but he wore a dark blue security jacket with "F.B.I." across its back. The lettering caused Klewe to wonder aloud why this person was keeping his distance from an investigation everyone else wanted to lead. As soon as he'd said that, Zelda let go of his arm.

"There's Officer Cooper," Zelda pointed to the Crown Victoria parked on the distant edge of the driveway. "I think he's leaving."

Klewe walked briskly over to the gray Ford to retrieve his umbrella from the young officer. He turned back to see Zelda taking notes as she spoke with the man beside the sculpture. As Klewe strode toward them, the man dropped his cigarette and ambled down the hill away from Kennedy Center.

"Was he really F.B.I.?" Klewe asked, coming up to Zelda.

"Not the one you're thinking," she sighed, quickly closing her notebook. "Foggy Bottom Investigations. Name tag said Hal Iger, a security officer who works near here. He had, well, some unique insights into the case."

"Like what?"

Failing to answer him, Zelda peered through the growing dusk and recognized that the sculpture near them was a metallic rendering of Don Quixote atop his horse Rocinante. After sizing up the post-modern artwork, meant as a tribute to the Spanish author Miguel de Cervantes, she elbowed Klewe unceremoniously in the side. "So did you give me the right answer at the Folger?"

He looked back at her, his eyes uncomprehending.

"To my crossword puzzle. Great writer who died in 1616, same date but not same day as Shakespeare. Nine letters, starting with C."

"Oh, yes. Cervantes."

"Really? The author of 'Don Quixote'?"

Klewe took stock of the sculpture, which was Spain's gift to Kennedy Center for the Bicentennial, and nodded.

"But how can that be?" Zelda asked. "'Same date but not same day'—it sounds impossible."

"Not really. Both Cervantes and Shakespeare were said to have died on the 23rd day of April in 1616. By that year Spain had already adopted the Gregorian calendar of the Catholic Church, while England still used the Julian calendar until the next century. That's how two writers could die on the same date, even though it was actually days apart."

Klewe turned his gaze back to Zelda.

"What about Hal Iger?" he insisted. "Did he tell you anything useful?"

"Sure did," Zelda responded with a dubious glint in her eye. "Claims he even witnessed the murder."

"What? Has he told the police?"

"Yeah, but they didn't take him too seriously. He said he was close enough to hear what the killer said. Even saw him when the killer's hood slipped."

"So why didn't they believe him?"

"Probably his choice of suspect," Zelda said, reading from her notes. "He said Shakespeare did it."

"I see." Klewe stifled a smile. They both stared downhill at Iger as he wound an unsteady path through the traffic on Virginia Avenue. "Sounds like somebody's been enjoying his Halloween a little too much."

"You're right." Zelda folded up her notebook. "I could smell Scotch yards away."

"Might as well be going. I already told Officer Cooper we could find our own way back to the Folger."

"But shouldn't we pass along this new information?"

"What information? That some guy who was most likely drunk thought he saw Shakespeare commit a murder? I think Detective Robinson has heard enough strange stories out of me for one day, thank you."

They walked away from the Quixote sculpture and followed the downhill route taken by the security guard, who was no longer in their view. They crossed a side street and stopped next to the Watergate, the circular hotel complex famed for its role in Richard Nixon's downfall from the White House.

Klewe watched as Zelda approached the tall gray exterior of the Watergate. Lifting a hand to caress its surface, she said, "This place is sacred. Holy for journalists, you know. I wasn't even born when all of that happened, but it still inspires me. Sort of my power source, where I can plug back in." She thought for a moment. "What's yours? I mean, your power source for Shakespeare? The Globe Theater, I guess."

"Or else his hometown of Stratford-upon-Avon. That's the place most Bardophiles visit. To see his grave, as you said."

Remembering her gift, he pulled the glass ornament containing the dried clover from his pocket and fingered it, his eyes taking in her reaction. "For luck, right?"

"That's why I gave it to you. For good luck."

"Yes, good luck."

They walked on, skirting the extended Watergate complex as they went. A doorman eyed their presence suspiciously until they had completely cleared the driveway and reached the next street corner. There they awaited a walk signal toward the nearest Metro station. With nighttime settling in, they could see they were approaching narrower streets lined with trees and restored townhouses, some dimly lit by the candles of carved pumpkins on stoops or inside front windows.

Once the light changed, they cautiously crossed over several lanes of Virginia Avenue. Nobody else was on foot near them, at least not until the red hand of the walk signal began blinking furiously. Then Klewe glanced back over his shoulder to discern a man in a rain slicker hurrying along behind them.

Klewe directed Zelda to turn at the corner of 24th Street. When the man behind them made the same turn, however, Klewe felt a twinge of alarm and increased their pace.

"What's going on?" Zelda asked, trying to turn around.

"Keep walking," he replied, "and don't look back."

They kicked at wet leaves as they rounded a corner and could see the clustered buildings of George Washington University ahead. On the western edge of campus, a tall brown pylon marked the Foggy Bottom entrance to Washington's Metrorail system, and they rushed toward the sign.

A traffic light ahead glowed red, forcing them to wait for a stream of cars. A small group of young G.W. students, on their way to evening classes, paused alongside them for the light to change. When Klewe looked back for the shadowy figure, he could no longer see the man there.

"You think the killer really looked like Shakespeare?" Zelda asked him suddenly.

Klewe tapped his foot, trying unsuccessfully to induce the walk cycle to come faster. "How does Shakespeare look?" was all he said.

When the light finally changed, the group entered the intersection together. At their feet lay the remains of a broken pumpkin, which they cautiously sidestepped. Then Klewe turned again and saw the stranger, now much closer to them.

"We're being followed," he told her sharply. "He's right behind us."

"Has he said anything?"

"Like what?"

"Hal Iger said the killer kept repeating something. 'We make his praise' or 'We all praise him,' something like that."

He stopped short and looked at her. "You mean 'We all make his praise'?"

"That's it. Does it mean something?"

They started forward again at a faster pace. "It's an anagram."

"Of what?" Zelda inquired. By now, they had reached the street corner nearest the Metro station. Both of them were breathing harder as they raced toward the entrance and ran down the moving steps of a lengthy escalator.

"I'll tell you," he said, "once we're onboard."

They quickly fed dollar bills into an automatic fare machine to receive two cards. From where they were standing below street level, they could see the hem of the rain slicker as the man descended the escalator toward them, and they hurried into the system.

The Metro turnstiles buzzed open after they inserted their fare cards, and the two dodged down a shorter escalator leading to the train platform. There an eastbound train was already entering the underground station, lights flashing along the platform to indicate its arrival.

Zelda stopped Klewe unexpectedly as the metal doors opened. "Can it really be true Shakespeare was black?" she asked him. "Wouldn't somebody have said something about it at the time?"

"Somebody did," he said, trying to urge her forward through the train door. "It was what another writer called him when Shakespeare first became successful in the London theater."

"What's that?"

"An upstart crow."

Zelda turned to give him a sharp stare, and they fell backward together into the train as the Metro doors slid shut behind them.

Chapter 8.

TO THEIR CONSTERNATION, however, the Metro doors immediately bounced back and remained wide open.

"This way!" Zelda snatched at the sleeve of Klewe's blazer to draw him along the narrow aisle inside the train car. Dozens of riders had filled the rush-hour seats, but there was still room enough to pass between the short benches. At last they heard the doors closing.

Each of them grabbed for a floor-to-ceiling pole while the train twisted its way into the next part of the tunnel. As they made their way to the front of the Blue Line car, Klewe tried to tell if the man was still following them. He kept his head low at the next stop, but soon realized their pursuer would now be harder to recognize, merely another face in a torrent of commuters on their way home. The doors slid shut again, and the train glided toward its main downtown stop.

"We have to decide what to do at Metro Center," Klewe informed her. "We can stay on this train for the Folger. Or we can transfer to a Red Line train into Maryland."

"Why Maryland?"

"That's where Mason lived. Way out in the country. I doubt the police have found his house yet, much less investigated it. If there's a copy of the flash drive to be found, it's probably there."

The train came to its stop at Metro Center, and the doors opened wide. With a more determined yank at his coat sleeve, she had Klewe join her in the stream of passengers exiting the train.

They flowed along with the crowd through the open door and along the platform to the first escalator heading up to the next level. At the top of the escalator, they made a sharp turnabout and lined up among commuters waiting at another track.

A Red Line train hurtled up the track before them, and they lunged through the doors of the final car that arrived. In a matter of seconds, the loudspeaker announced the next stop, followed by two chimes to signal the closing of the doors. They found a row of empty benches and collapsed into two seats facing forward. Directly behind them sat a couple of teenage vampires that Klewe sincerely hoped were heading for a Halloween party. Also intermingled with commuters in business attire were several pirates and a Princess Leia.

"I hope we're going the right way," Zelda said, and Klewe craned his neck to see the map posted inside the car.

"Red Line for Shady Grove," the announcer called out just then. "Next stop Farragut North."

"We're all right here if we're alone," he said, then realized how odd that sounded amid a swarm of people. "I meant, if he's not here."

"I know what you meant. Come on."

Zelda was back on her feet and motioning for Klewe to go with her. At the extreme front of their car, a pair of seats across from each other had opened up, allowing them to sit facing each other and have clear views in both directions. They settled into the seats, leaning forward to continue their conversation across the aisle.

"I've been on the Red Line before," she said, "just not all the way to the end."

"That'll be the Shady Grove station. It's the nearest stop in Montgomery County to Mason's cabin."

"Cabin?"

"I told you it's way out in the countryside."

"Can't wait. But what I really want to know about is the anagram."

"You're a writer," he said, lifting a pen from his pocket and picking up a discarded newspaper from a nearby seat, "so you know how easily letters in words can be rearranged for other words."

"I know what anagrams are, Professor. In fact, I could probably take you at a game of Scrabble. But what was the killer trying to say?"

"Here, I'll show you."

He paged randomly through the newspaper to find an empty white space and used the pen again. "Hal Iger told you the killer said, 'We all make his praise.' Anything look familiar about the 18 letters in those words?" He handed her the paper and the pen.

She studied the five words he'd written as the train glided along. From overhead, she could hear that the next stop would be Tenleytown near American University but redoubled her efforts to concentrate on solving the puzzle before her. Blowing hair out of her eyes with frustration, she gave up and handed him back the page.

Klewe filled in a second line beneath the words he had already written and returned the paper. Her eyes began to shine as she read the rearranged letters. First:

WE ALL MAKE HIS PRAISE.

And then:

WILLIAM SHAKESPEARE.

Chapter 9.

ZELDA SCRUPULOUSLY COUNTED the letters in both entries, drawing mental lines to corroborate the anagram. "Exactly 18 letters spelling out Shakespeare's name," she conceded. "But even if there is some dangerous conspiracy going on here, what are we supposed to do about it?"

"Not 'we,'" Klewe said. "I'm going to London to make that speech for Mason. I owe him that much."

"Oh, no, don't even think about leaving me behind."

"No, I don't suppose you'd let me do that. Before London, though, we need to see if Mason left a copy of his computer files at his house. I already have several chapters written, but he was handling all the research about racial difference in Elizabethan England. That was going to be his main contribution to our book."

"He was also examining portraits of Shakespeare?"

"Yes, while I looked into written references by Shakespeare's contemporaries. Of course, each generation since that time has tried guessing the Bard's secret. You wouldn't believe some of the bizarre theories about Shakespeare I've come across." She glared at him. "Okay, maybe you would."

Zelda turned back to consider the anagram again. "Isn't it false, though? Not everyone makes his praise. What about that Dead White Male business?"

"Well, that is true. George Bernard Shaw once wished they'd dig up Shakespeare's body so he could throw stones at it. And Ben Jonson wasn't always complimentary in Shakespeare's day, but at least Jonson didn't call him an 'upstart crow' in print."

"So who did?"

"It appeared in a 1592 pamphlet written by a dying man. A playwright named Robert Greene, whose work was popular in London before Shakespeare came to town and started stealing his thunder. Unfortunately, Greene saw the rising Shakespeare as a threat to his own career, so he talked a publisher, Henry Chettle, into printing his attack on the new writer in town. In his pamphlet, Greene also identified the Bard as 'the only Shake-scene in the country.' Believe it or not, literary critics have gone into contortions trying to prove that he meant somebody other than Shakespeare."

"That's silly. He wouldn't have used 'Shake-scene' if he wanted to insult somebody else. His readers could have missed the point entirely, couldn't they?"

"I agree. Besides, Greene also uses some dialogue out of an early history play by the Bard. In 'Henry the Sixth, Part Three,' Shakespeare wrote about a 'tiger's heart wrapped in a woman's hide.' Greene changed that to 'tiger's heart wrapped in a player's hide' for his insult. Back then Shakespeare was known as a player." At Zelda's slight smirk, he added, "Not what it means now. It meant he was an actor."

"And they still don't think Greene was referring to Shakespeare?"

"No, but it gets worse. There have been buckets of ink spilled trying to explain Robert Greene's use of the adjective 'upstart,' but a lot less attention paid to the noun 'crow.' That's what got me thinking about what was really being said."

"I take it 'upstart' was a strong insult back then?"

"Maybe so, but Greene had used it more than once to attack people he didn't like. His use of 'crow,' on the other hand, stands out in his words. And after Greene died, the publisher of the pamphlet went so far as to make a printed apology to Shakespeare for having maligned him."

"That does make you wonder."

"Think this through, as I like to tell my students. If you look up the definition of 'crow' in the Oxford English Dictionary, the greatest dictionary about the history of our language, you'll find the noun 'crow' with its literal use for the bird with black feathers. That's followed by figurative uses of the word applied to human beings. The first figurative example given is Greene's comment about Shakespeare, followed by more modern racist uses like 'Jim Crow.'"

They heard an announcement for the Grosvenor station next. At that moment they both twisted about, as other passengers did, to stare out the windows as the train came shooting up out of its tunnel to street level. On the raised track, they could now see they were parallel to Rockville Pike, where headlights speckled multiple lanes of traffic.

"We're heading through Bethesda," Zelda said.

"I know. I came out this way to visit Mason sometimes."

She gave him a smug smile. "But did you know this area has a famous literary tie to the fight against racism?"

"What's that?"

She settled back into her seat with triumph at her chance to teach the teacher. "This road next to us is Rockville Pike, and the next major street over is Old Georgetown Road."

"I've heard of it."

"Have you heard what building is located there?"

Klewe shook his head, and Zelda savored the moment.

"A small log house. It's joined to a bigger house now, but once it stood there by itself. Harriet Beecher Stowe used it as her inspiration for 'Uncle Tom's Cabin.'"

"In Maryland? I always thought that was in the Deep South."

"And that's not the only literary site to see around here. There's also this place coming up in Rockville I want you to—"

Klewe stopped her. "No time now, not till we're safe."

The last word resounded like a struck cymbal. The train came to a halt in the Rockville station, the penultimate stop of its run, and Zelda stood up to stretch her legs. As she did, she glanced casually away from Klewe and into the adjoining Metro car.

Klewe had faced the other way when he felt her staggering back against him. "What's the matter?" She didn't respond. "What is it?"

Pointing into the next car, she was trying to mouth something silently to him. He finally recognized the word. "Dagger."

Chapter 10.

"CHRISTOPHER?" ZELDA WAS pronouncing his name so softly that Klewe failed to notice the fear in her voice. It was the first time she had called him by his given name, and he found the familiarity appealing.

"Chris!"

This time she spoke sharply and turned to him with panicked eyes.

"What?"

She put out her hand for his umbrella, which he handed to her instantly. From above them, the loudspeaker crackled its reminder that riders should watch for the closing of the Metro doors, the announcement followed by the ringing of chimes. The exit began to slide shut, the two parts of the door coming together before the train could proceed.

Desperately, Zelda shoved the umbrella's curved wooden handle into the diminishing space in the doorway and tried using it for leverage. She held her breath tightly.

After a long instant, the door grudgingly gave way, opening wide again.

"Now!" Zelda ordered him urgently.

The audio warning repeated its message that "The doors are now closing." While the exit remained open, Zelda barely had long enough to seize a stunned Klewe and drag him off the train before the doors could close. They watched in tense silence while the train started to glide out of the Rockville station toward Shady Grove.

"What is wrong with you?"

"Shakespeare!" she exclaimed, gesturing frantically at the departing train. "High forehead, doe eyes, the same way he looks in that damn Folger book."

In vain Klewe struggled to glimpse whoever it was she had seen onboard. He gave up the effort and turned his attention to the outdoor Rockville platform where they now stood. Standing nearby were a handful of passengers, all with their backs turned to them, ready to take the next train inbound to Washington.

Their own Metro train, however, lurched forward several feet and came to an unexpected stop. Without waiting to see whether the doors would open again, Zelda took Klewe by the hand and onto an escalator. The moving stairs carried them down from the elevated platform to the main part of the station, where several riders were waiting their turn to exit through turnstiles.

The two of them joined the shortest line they could find and inserted their fare cards. Grudgingly the gates yielded, permitting them to leave the system. Without bothering to look back, they sprinted away from the Rockville station into darkness. At the distant edge of the station's parking lot, they saw cars lined up, idling to pick up commuters. They finally felt safe enough to slow their pace to a walk.

"It was Shakespeare, I tell you," Zelda kept insisting. "He stared straight at me. Waving a bloody dagger." She realized what she was saying and put a hand to her head. "The killer, I mean. Not Shakespeare. Somebody wearing his mask."

"How could he have followed us all this way?"

"I don't know." She wrenched herself about to check the station behind them. "You didn't see him?"

"No, but a guy in a mask really isn't going to attract very much attention on Halloween."

"What about a guy with a knife? And where do you think he got that mask?"

"Maybe the Folger. These days, though, it's not very difficult to look like Shakespeare, given how generic his look has become."

"At least we're off the train."

"Yes, but where? I've always ridden out to Shady Grove to meet Mason. This platform says Rockville."

Zelda saw one of the Metro signs and rapidly gained a sparkle in her eyes. "Oh, good. Now I can show you that literary landmark I'd mentioned."

With weariness more than trepidation, he began to follow her. They wandered through a corner of the Metro lot onto a back street and continued about a block from the station.

"It's over this way." She led him into an area overshadowed by trees and rows of tall shrubbery. Approaching a short circular building, he realized it was the side entrance to a church, with a prominent sign identifying it as St. Mary's Catholic. Rather than entering the church proper, however, they veered off to one side, into the darkness of a small cemetery. The graveyard extended from where they stood to the very edge of Rockville Pike, a roadway full of cars racing past them.

Zelda eagerly directed Klewe along a small walkway near the door of the church and stopped him in front of a long flat stone with a headstone above it. "There."

"Where? What are you showing me?"

"The stone." She withdrew a tiny flashlight from the lower depths of her shoulder bag. "You may need this."

The beam caught the edge of a name on the upright stone, and he began to read. The first word he found was "Zelda," but she directed him to keep the light moving along. Francis Scott Key and Zelda Sayre were the two names listed on the Fitzgerald headstone. When he realized the significance, he looked sharply up at her.

"Are you serious? Is this where F. Scott Fitzgerald and his wife are buried?"

"Not the original grave. The Catholic Church wouldn't allow him to be buried in holy ground at first, calling his writings 'undesirable.' Later, though, he and Zelda were buried together here."

"Their final resting place."

"I suppose," she hesitated, "it's as final as anyone can say a resting place will be."

Klewe stood upright. "I'll bet you were named for her."

Zelda smiled broadly. "My grandmother was, and then I was named Zelda Joan Hart for her. My mother always said I had writer's blood in me." She looked down again at the tombstone. "Can you believe these two were almost denied a churchyard burial?"

"People don't like their religious traditions to be challenged. There was a time a generation ago when a lot of white Christians were upset to hear the media suggesting that Jesus was black."

"Which may well be true, but how would you ever prove it one way or the other?"

"Short of time travel, it's not likely. The bigger issue is why it would matter anyway."

"It really shouldn't." Zelda thought for a moment. "On the other hand, the historical Jesus lived two thousand years ago. Wouldn't it be a whole lot easier to find out about someone from a later time like Shakespeare?"

"You'd think so." Klewe rubbed his chilled fingers together. "But the same thing has happened to other writers, more recent ones than Shakespeare."

"Who?"

"There's been debate about whether Robert Browning and Elizabeth Barrett Browning were black, two of England's greatest poets, and they lived in the 19th century. Each had family ties to Jamaica that could have been interracial, and they say you can easily tell about Browning's ancestry by looking at his portraits. And are you familiar with Alexander Pushkin?"

"I've heard of him. Russian, I think."

"Yes, he was also a 19th-century poet. He became known as the Russian Shakespeare." He gave a sly smile. "There may be more truth there than was intended."

"But most people probably have no idea what the Brownings or Pushkin looked like."

"And those authors lived less than two centuries ago. We do know that people of one race can sometimes pass for another, as TV talk shows often point out, especially people with a biracial background."

Zelda looked skeptical.

"Hey," he continued, "you said yourself that we picture him with a high forehead and doe eyes. But who knows whether Shakespeare had either of those characteristics? Four centuries after he died, we all feel like we know Shakespeare—hell, even Bill Clinton called him 'old Will' in his autobiography—but we can't really be sure of what he looked like. If Shakespeare was biracial, things may have been done to keep that fact hidden."

The cemetery itself had grown eerily quiet for its proximity to Rockville Pike. There were no other graveyard visitors, so Zelda took back her small flashlight. She pointed the beam downward to the large flat stone to reveal lettering across its surface.

Klewe leaned over to read the rain-dampened print on the horizontal stone. "What does that say?" He began to read carefully, "'So we beat on, boats against the current, borne back ceaselessly into the past.'"

"The final line of 'The Great Gatsby.' I've always loved that novel."

She had no sooner said that than they heard footsteps coming close to them and instinctively huddled together. Reaching out to Klewe, Zelda lost her balance on the wet surface, causing her to tumble backward onto the hard stone. And as she fell, her hand clutched Klewe's arm, awkwardly tugging him down until his body landed flat atop hers on the gravestone.

THE SECOND ACT:
UPSTART CROW

Chapter 11.

AT THE EDGE of St. Mary's cemetery, the clatter of footsteps resounded firmly on pavement in the misty night air. Then the noise clearly shifted, heading away from the graveyard. Klewe and Zelda rose to their feet, dusting themselves off. In the receding shadows, they could make out a portly man grasping the leash to restrain a nervously energetic greyhound on their nightly walk. Farther along, they could see costumed children darting along the street in the final throes of trick-or-treating.

"Did you know," she asked to fight off her embarrassment, "that Scott and Zelda were buried one on top of the other? I've heard that these days lovers have sometimes sought out this very spot to be together."

Klewe leveled his gaze into her eyes.

"Have I shocked you?" she teased him. "I suppose some people would find that offensive, but I have a feeling Scott and Zelda don't mind."

"I don't shock easily," he replied. "But we do need to get going. Shall we beat on?"

"Boats against the current," she agreed, and they walked back to the streetlights that bordered St. Mary's.

At the corner, Klewe stopped uncertainly. "Do we try Metro again?"

Zelda's brow furrowed. "I don't think so."

"Then what?"

"Here's an idea." She stepped off the curb and lifted her hand toward the Rockville station. "Taxi!"

Klewe followed sheepishly behind, as a smirking Zelda signaled to the lead cab in the Metro line. Its driver, brushing back flat strands of white hair on his forehead, revved the engine as they jumped into the back seat.

"Good idea," Klewe told her, giving in to a reluctant smile. He informed the driver, "We're heading to Sugarloaf Mountain." The taxi shot away from the curb as the cabbie grunted with irritation. "That should put us close to Mason's place."

"How far is it?"

"Twenty miles or so."

"Good. You can tell me more about this theory of yours." She made a quick assessment of the driver, who appeared to be concentrating solely on his radio, and turned her attention to Klewe. "Who else described Shakespeare besides that Greene guy?"

He considered where to start. "There are other contemporary references to how Shakespeare looked, but only two of them. One you probably haven't even heard of, because very few people have, but there was a popular poem written about the funeral of Queen Elizabeth. We're talking the first Queen Elizabeth, the one who died in 1603. The poem was written by Henry Chettle, the same guy who printed Greene's pamphlet about the 'upstart crow.'"

"And later apologized for printing it."

"Right. Anyway, when Elizabeth passed away, Chettle penned an elegy about the death of the great monarch, and in it he described how several different poets failed to express enough grief at the loss of England's Virgin Queen. When Chettle came to Shakespeare, though, he used a phrase not found anywhere else in the poem."

"What was that?"

"He wrote that Shakespeare did not seem to shed a 'sable tear.' The word 'sable' was used back then, as it still is, for the darkness of animal fur. It's basically a synonym for 'black.'"

"Sable? Does Chettle say anything else about him?"

"No, but why do you think color was considered important in a description for Shakespeare and none of the other mourners in the poem?"

"I see what you're saying. Why would Shakespeare be the only one singled out that way unless the writer wanted to convey there was something different about him?"

"Precisely. And then we have the other comment, which was made by the most astute writer about how Shakespeare looked."

"Who's that?"

"Shakespeare himself," Klewe said. "Readers have combed through his plays and sonnets for the past four centuries, determined to find information about him. For example, he describes himself in Sonnet 37 as being lame, so scholars have wondered if he was physically deformed or had trouble walking. Meanwhile, they don't even notice Sonnet 62 where he describes his old age as 'tanned antiquity.' It's the only place he uses the adjective 'tanned' in referring to himself."

Zelda watched him thoughtfully. "And 'tanned' would suggest a darker skin color than others around him had."

"That's it. So we have 'sable' and 'tanned.' Those two, along with the 'upstart crow' reference, make up the three—the only three—comments about Shakespeare's physical appearance during his lifetime by people who had seen him and known him."

They felt a series of gentle jolts as the cab proceeded along Route 28 into northern Montgomery County. As they neared their destination, Klewe withdrew his wallet and found only a few dollars inside. He turned to Zelda, who shrugged at him.

"Sir," he asked the driver, "do you take credit cards?" A cursory nod was the entire response.

Klewe removed a Visa card from his wallet. The cab was skirting dimly lit orchards, with long lines of close-set trees scattered between open fields and occasional farmhouses. After spotting a sign for Peachtree Road, Klewe asked the driver to take a right and go another mile. They slowed to a stop at a gravel driveway near a row of mailboxes.

"This will do." Klewe waited for the driver to process his Visa and reluctantly signed the receipt. "Can you wait for us?"

"Not out here," the driver said coldly. By the time the pair had climbed out and shut the door, he was already starting his three-point turn back onto the road. When the lights of the taxi disappeared over the rise, they realized how dark the Maryland night had become.

"Why did you look so concerned about paying him?" Zelda asked Klewe.

"The credit card. Now there's an electronic record of where we are. We'd better move along before someone finds us."

"Here's my flashlight. You lead the way."

They started down a dirt road as it curved around a farmhouse that seemed empty. Suddenly they heard the sharp bark of a tethered German shepherd. Both of them jumped at the unexpected noise but kept walking.

Finally, Zelda said, "Were there any other insults directed at Shakespeare?"

He pitched the beam of the flashlight before them as they trudged along the damp terrain. "I believe there was one, a popular Elizabethan play titled 'Arden of Faversham.' It was written about the time Shakespeare was making his name in London. In the play, which was based on an actual crime, Arden is a nasty guy whose wife hires two killers to get rid of him."

"I love a good murder mystery."

"Sadly for the wife, though, her plans keep getting messed up, at least until the bloody climax. For a long time, people assumed Shakespeare had written it, but now the author is usually listed as 'Anonymous,' like the name of that movie where Shakespeare wasn't the Bard. I personally think 'Arden of Faversham' was meant to be another swipe at Shakespeare."

"What makes you think so?"

"The name Arden. That was the maiden name of his Catholic mother, Mary Arden Shakespeare, and he used the Forest of Arden in 'As You Like It.'"

"Was that the only connection?"

"No. Then we have the names of the two incompetent killers in 'Arden of Faversham.' The first one was called Shake-bag."

"That's about as subtle as Shake-scene was. What was the other killer's name?"

He took a deep breath. "Black Will."

"No shit!" Zelda stopped dead in her tracks, but Klewe kept walking with the flashlight. She scurried in the darkness to catch up with him.

The next thing he heard was a heavy thud, followed by a splashing noise. He pivoted the flashlight to see Zelda slogging her way out of a deep mud puddle in the middle of the road. She came up to him, her hands flinging water and wiping mud from her jacket. He stared blankly at her, saying nothing.

"My hero!" she snapped at last.

"It can't be," he stammered to himself, "it just can't be." He allowed the beam of light to stray aimlessly from the ground. "If that's what Mason meant ..."

Klewe let his thought trail off. As he twisted about to look back for signs they were being followed, he made only one other comment Zelda could hear.

"God help us."

Chapter 12.

THE CLOUD COVER hanging above them had started pulling clumsily apart like overworked taffy, allowing moonlight to streak through in a dazzling display of rays and mist. Zelda, however, was appreciating none of it, standing there in the rutted road while the mud on her windbreaker dripped steadily onto her boots.

Klewe maintained his stunned silence amid the night's drone of crickets and katydids. When he shook himself back to the moment, he placed a concerned hand on her sleeve and wiped away some of the mud.

"I'm so sorry. Are you all right?" He removed his blue blazer to wrap around her and then offered her the flashlight. Using the closed umbrella as a walking stick, he slowly secured their footing along the winding driveway. Ahead they could see the outline of a short dark building, a wet blur that resolved itself as they came closer into the exterior of a log cabin. "Hold on a minute."

Klewe took back the flashlight as they stood at the entrance. After running the beam across a series of rocks near the door, he lifted the smallest stone to uncover a house key. "Let's get inside." He inserted the key and nudged the heavy timbered door with his shoulder. Then he fumbled in the darkness for a wall switch, flooding the inside of the log cabin with electric light. "Better?"

"Yes." She returned the blazer to him. "Sorry I snapped at you out there. I'm not somebody who's big on chivalry anyway."

"Let's just be thankful Mason showed me where he hid the key."

"So I guess we're technically not breaking, only entering." She ran her hand across the roughhewn logs of an inside wall, some of which sported J.M.U. pennants, and then examined the polished hardwood floor. "And what's that over there?"

Zelda walked over to an enormous map affixed to the logs. Laying out the street patterns of the District of Columbia in giant detail, the map covered almost an entire wall of the small cabin.

"As you can see, Mason loved Washington. The architecture, the history, the whole nine yards. That's why he and Amanda moved here from Harrisonburg a few years ago when they retired, but it also may have been one of the reasons they split up. She told me Mason was spending more time downtown than with her, so she left him and took a place up the road in Frederick." He grew reflective. "God, how will I tell Ammie?"

"You'll find the words." She eyed herself suspiciously in a wall mirror. "Any place around here I might clean up a little?"

"Sure." He pointed her to a door on the far side of the log room. "They built onto the original cabin and updated everything. You'll find a bathroom through the door there, and beyond that a kitchen area and the bedroom."

"All in logs?" She smiled at him.

"No, those are much more modern. Indoor plumbing too." He smiled back. "Make yourself comfortable." Klewe caught himself before adding that his colleague wouldn't mind.

She excused herself for a few minutes. He could hear her moving about in the other part of the house as he examined the cabin area. One corner held a work station, its desk and cabinet stacked with books as well as files to be sorted. He shuffled through some of the papers, but nothing drew his attention.

Instead, he examined the computer atop the desk, but there was no flash drive. After pressing a few buttons, he waited for the monitor's screen to light up.

"I hope it's all right," Zelda called from the back room. "There's a heat lamp in the bathroom, so I'm using it to dry out my clothes."

"Fine, whatever you need. Is the place too rustic for you?"

She entered the cabin again, folding back the raglan sleeves of a loose-fitting bathrobe she'd found. "Not me. I grew up in a place like this."

"Really? I thought you were a city girl."

"Nope, born and raised in West Virginia. Until I could escape to college."

"Tell me about it." He invited her to join him astride a long couch that faced the wall map.

"Wouldn't you rather hear some music?" She found a soft jazz station on a table-top radio and let it play quietly in the background. Then, as she settled onto the couch, the white bathrobe she was wearing started to drop open. Zelda grabbed at the material and pulled it tightly back together. "Hold on, I'm having a Janet Jackson moment here."

"So I see."

"Hey, I thought music was supposed to soothe the savage beast."

"That's not 'beast,' it's 'breast,'" he corrected her in a professorial tone and then stopped, embarrassed.

"So you see," she said playfully, watching his reaction. "That's very sexy. I'm glad to see there are still some men who can blush." Klewe did not reply. The long robe covered her pale feet as she drew her legs under her on the couch. "Anyway, enough about me. Tell me what you figured out while I took my mud bath outside here."

After checking the computer's progress, he switched off the music and walked back to the couch, seating himself next to her. He gazed directly into her eyes, his tone deadly serious.

"Have you ever heard," he asked her diffidently, "of the School of Night?"

Chapter 13.

ZELDA FROWNED AT the question. "You mean night school?"

"No," Klewe insisted. "The School of Night."

She determinedly shook her head. The brittle silence in the room intensified, and they could hear the wind outside, with cold air struggling to filter its way into the cabin. As Klewe began to talk, she made nervous twists of the wedding band on her finger.

"That's what Mason was trying to tell me. He wrote those initials for it on the glass at Kennedy Center, but I didn't know what he meant." He paused. "Maybe I didn't want to know."

Klewe could tell she was trembling and wrapped a duvet from the back of the couch around her robed figure.

"Is it an actual school?"

"The School of Night was a name given to a secret society that originated in England back in Shakespeare's day. A group of wealthy, educated men who met clandestinely to share dangerous ideas, even seditious ones. It was supposedly a breeding ground for atheists, but Elizabeth's government prosecuted anti-Protestant thoughts as heresy, punishable by the most brutal of tortures."

Zelda shivered again, but said nothing as he continued.

"Not much is known for certain, but it's thought to have been started by the man we know as Sir Walter Raleigh—back then his name was pronounced like 'water rawly'—along with a small circle of intimates. Nobody really knows what its true purpose was or how many members there were. But to be recognized as a member of such a group would most likely have resulted in imprisonment, if not death."

"Did Shakespeare belong to this school?"

"That much we don't know, but I don't think so." Klewe rose from the couch and circled behind it to retrieve a volume from a long shelf against the wall. As he opened the book, she saw it was a collection of Shakespeare's plays. "What he did, though, was to leave us an enduring mention of the school's existence. It was known at the time as the School of Atheism, but Shakespeare changed that by writing a few lines into 'Love's Labor's Lost.'"

"That's one of his comedies, right?"

"Yes, an early one. In the play, the King of Navarre is talking with his follower Berowne about the paradox of how black can be beautiful despite having negative connotations. 'Black is the badge of hell,' the King says. 'The hue of dungeons and the school of night.'" Klewe closed the volume. "Hell, dungeons and the School of Night, all being painted with the same brush. Not exactly a favorable picture of that group. In fact, making fun of them may have been the Bard's undoing by Raleigh and cohorts."

"How do you mean?"

"Say that our theory is right, just for argument's sake. How much do you think a biracial playwright, particularly a genius, would have been appreciated by an almost exclusively white society? Especially by men of noble birth and wealthy means."

"That's not very hard to figure out."

"So what would happen if he were a target of that group? Even if they decided to tolerate him during his lifetime, what kind of legacy would they permit him to leave?"

"Not much of one, I'd imagine."

"You're right. They would have done whatever they could to cover up the truth about him. Raleigh's followers would already have had money and influence, the two most important elements needed if they wanted to spread prejudice and racism."

He paused again before going on.

"Shakespeare was living in a time that was especially danger-ous for any secret societies that the monarchy disapproved of. We have records of some of the bloodiest murders committed in the name of Elizabeth's crown. And atheists were among the most suspect of criminals back then. In Renaissance England, for exam-ple, it was considered treasonous to use 'Dog' as the backward spelling of 'God.' Proof positive that you were an atheist and de-served death. But not just killed. Hanged, then cut down alive so you could have your intestines removed to see before you died."

Klewe replaced the book on its shelf and turned back to Zelda.

"Over the years, there have been lots of books and persistent rumors about the true meaning of this School of Night. Nobody can say with certainty if it died out or if it's still around. All we know is that Raleigh's group started something that has caused four centuries of curiosity and fear. And Shakespeare put them on pub-lic notice with one of his plays that he wasn't afraid to speak out about them."

Zelda inhaled deeply, trying to shake the troubling images of torture and death from her mind.

"Hold on a minute," she said, rubbing her hands against the bathrobe. "There's no evidence of their continued existence, you said. Then who's trying to kill us?"

"There's no conclusive evidence, but hate seems to be a force capable of sustaining itself over long periods of time. And what if the School of Night is still around, as some people think—if it was formed to practice racism, wouldn't it be just as effective today as it was in Elizabethan England?"

"So you think Mason died trying to warn you about the School of Night?"

"I didn't realize it until you took that spill in the driveway. Then the meaning became obvious."

"Not to me."

"Well, what do you know about Sir Walter Raleigh?"

"Not that much. He was an explorer who liked to smoke tobacco. He's also the one who brought back the potato from the New World. And didn't he spend a lot of his time in prison?"

"Before he was beheaded. He was also a true courtier, which meant he was often in the Queen's company and practiced courtly manners."

"That's right. Isn't he the guy who laid his cloak across a puddle so the Queen wouldn't get her feet wet?" Zelda's eyes filled exuberantly with recognition. "Mason's raincoat! He spread it over that puddle to point you to Raleigh, didn't he?"

Klewe lowered his head solemnly to consider. "Mason wanted to identify the group who killed him. And, as Detective Robinson so delicately put it, I may be next." He scrupulously avoided saying, "And you too," but he knew she got the implication.

Klewe said nothing more, suddenly turning all his attention toward the front door. He put up his hand for Zelda to keep still.

Outside the remote Maryland cabin, the silence of the nighttime was being broken by the unmistakable sound of a car slowly rounding the driveway and coming to a stop near the front door.

Chapter 14.

THE HIGH BEAMS of headlights bore two brilliant holes through the narrow window of the cabin door. Klewe jumped up to kill the inside lights at the wall switch.

"Behind the couch!" he urged from the threshold, wildly directing Zelda to protect herself.

A car door outside was softly closed, followed by what seemed an excessively long stillness. At last the knob on the oak door began to turn ever so slightly, and the door yielded with a loud creaking noise. Zelda could hear a clash of bodies rushing together in the dark, followed by a short outcry from somebody striking the floor.

She reached soundlessly for the wall switch and turned on the light again.

Klewe lay awkwardly at her feet, his chest pinned to the ground by a long muddied boot. Wearing the boot, and looking as anxious as both of them, was a thin older woman in rain gear. The woman pulled a fisherman's hat from her long gray hair before lifting her foot and spitting out a question at him.

"Christopher, is that you?"

More shaken than injured, he sat halfway up and stared at the victorious intruder. "I didn't know who you were," he managed to say. Hardly winded from their physical encounter, the woman stooped to offer him a hand, lifting him back to his feet.

"I should hope not," she said. "And please don't take this the wrong way, but what the hell are you doing here?"

He indicated the younger woman with him, who was trying hard not to laugh, and offered an introduction. "Ammie, this is Zelda Hart, a reporter. And, Zelda, here is my good friend, although you might not think so at the moment, Amanda Everly."

"Oh." Zelda took Amanda's hand. "Mason's wife?"

"I was. I don't live here anymore, but we've stayed friends. I even look after this place for him when he's away." She turned back to Klewe, who was still looking like damaged goods from their brief scuffle, and eyed him questioningly. "That's why I'm here in the middle of the night. A neighbor called to say there were lights on."

Klewe rubbed a bruised elbow. "Sorry if we scared you. I guess we made ourselves at home."

"Mason phoned yesterday to say he was coming back from Europe. Sounded excited by something he'd found for your new project."

Klewe wandered back to the computer and examined the screen. "Maybe you can help us with that. Ammie," he explained to Zelda, "is a computer wizard."

"Computer wiccan," Amanda corrected him. "So where is Mason? I didn't see his car outside." Klewe could not bring himself to answer. "Where's Mason gone this time, Chris? And why did you turn off the lights when I came in?"

"Come sit down, Ammie." He guided her gently toward the couch. She could tell the news would not be good and felt her legs beginning to give way. But she did not sit down, nor did she take her eyes from Klewe.

"What's wrong?"

"Something awful has happened. Mason's dead."

Amanda righted herself against the couch as she tried to process the information. Without saying a word, she sat down, awaiting the details. Zelda couldn't stop staring into the older woman's expressive eyes.

Klewe recounted the day's events, from the police visit at the Folger to the investigation at Kennedy Center. He left out the clues at the murder scene and their frenzied trip to the cabin. When he had finished, Amanda rose wordlessly from the couch and headed for the bedroom.

"Ammie? Is there anything we can do?"

She said nothing to him as she left the room and closed the door behind her.

"Give her a little while," Zelda suggested.

"I never meant to drag her into this."

"She's already in. More than she wants to be."

"You may be right." He went back to the computer and struck random keys that failed to generate anything of interest.

Zelda came over beside him and said consolingly, "It's a terrible loss for both of you."

"And here I am trying to make sense of it or make something good come out of it. I shouldn't even be asking her for help, but we need to find out what happened to Mason. I owe him that much. And Ammie can probably help if she's up to it."

"I am." Amanda came from the bedroom with a small bottle of Tylenol in hand. "You know, it's not funny exactly, but I've been thinking for days that something bad was about to happen." She wrestled with the childproof cap and finally succeeded in opening the bottle. With a quick thrust, she tossed back two capsules and swallowed hard without water. "You and your damned theory." She shook her head willfully at Klewe, then wandered back into the kitchen. With her back to them, she found an empty glass and absentmindedly rinsed it at the sink.

When Amanda emerged from the kitchen a moment later, she seemed more composed, perhaps a little too much in control. She slowly surveyed the cabin that she had once shared with her ex-husband, then looked around at them.

"Are those your things in the bathroom?" she inquired of Zelda, who grabbed self-consciously again at the neck of the white robe.

"I'm so sorry. I took a fall on the way in here tonight."

Amanda waved away the apologies. "You're all right?" she asked, retracing her steps to the kitchen. "I should offer you both something. Maybe something to eat?"

"No," they said in unison, although Zelda's hand went instantly to her empty stomach.

"Some tea then." They could hear the sound of a kettle being filled with water.

"She's really something," Zelda said admiringly. "Worried about us when she must feel like hell herself."

"Ammie's all that and more. I had been hoping she and Mason would—well, you know."

"What can we do for her?"

"I don't know. Except for finding out who did this to Mason."

When Klewe looked up, he found Amanda standing immediately in front of him. She had crossed the cabin floor without a sound. Her face was flushed, but he could tell she was not allowing herself to cry, determined to find answers.

"I need you to tell me something."

"Anything."

"The truth, Christopher." Amanda took a deep breath before she continued. "Was it the School of Night?"

Chapter 15.

KLEWE WISHED HE could lie to Amanda. Instead, he tried to evade her stare while answering indirectly. "Why do you say that?"

"Mason told me they'd made threats. He called a few times from Europe and tried to tell me about them, but I wasn't paying much attention. We had also been talking about reconciliation, so I was thinking about that."

He moved to put his arms around her.

"You know he loved you, Am." The statement was heartfelt by Klewe, and it almost produced tears in Amanda.

"Yes. And now they've killed him."

"The D.C. police are looking into it," Zelda told her.

"It was the School of Night, wasn't it?" Amanda persisted. "That's what he told me might happen. When he called from London, he said something about dangerous situations the last few days. But then he announced he was coming back here, and I never heard anything else from him."

Klewe wondered, "What kind of situations?"

"I can't say exactly, but I could hear the concern in his voice. Couldn't you hear it too?"

"Whenever he called me, everything sounded fine with him."

"That was Mason," Amanda conceded. "Didn't want you to worry about him. And nothing could make him stop working."

"I should have known, though. I should have realized something was off." He took Amanda's hand. "But he'd worked so hard on this new project. That's why I wanted him to make our big announcement this week at the Globe, and he seemed so eager to do it. I never picked up on the danger." She rubbed his hand comfortingly. "Had he said anything more about why he decided to leave London and come back here?"

Amanda thought for a minute. "He told me he was going to Paris to meet someone who had information for him. I asked what it was, but he said we'd talk when he got here." She looked desolately about the cabin and waited to catch her breath. "I told him to be careful. And then he said the strangest thing."

"What's that?"

"I'm not sure I can repeat it correctly. He said something about bird watching."

"I didn't know he was into that."

"Me neither. We live in the country, so he would sometimes tell me if he'd spotted a cardinal or a woodpecker, but I had never heard of this species. He said he was looking for a white crow."

Klewe was perplexed. "Are you sure he didn't say he was looking into Shakespeare's being called an upstart crow?"

"No, it was clearly a white crow. And he gave that nervous laugh he'd use when something really bothered him. A white crow." She gave an involuntary shiver. From the kitchen stove came the whistle of the kettle, but Zelda signaled her to stay.

"Let me get it. And I'll see if my clothes are dry."

Distractedly, Amanda sat back down beside him. "Did you say it was at Kennedy Center?"

"Early this afternoon."

She rolled her eyes. "That damn walking tour, I bet. Was he taking it again?"

"I don't really know."

She went to the computer and clicked the Internet browser. "They have a virtual tour on here, but he can't do that. No, he has to walk the actual steps, he says."

Klewe followed her to the screen. After a quick interlude of keystrokes, she had entered the Kennedy Center website and found the virtual tour.

"Where did it happen?" she asked.

"I'm not sure you should—"

"Show me where." She angled the monitor toward him.

He seated himself before the computer and began his usual hunt-and-peck routine to find the information he wanted. After a moment or two, the monitor showed the giant bronze bust of John Fitzgerald Kennedy's face.

"Next to this. The J.F.K. sculpture."

"Yes, I know that one. It faces the Opera House."

He stood up. "I need your help to find out why this happened."

"I want to know too."

He reached for a desk pen and an empty pad. After he wrote "N35" and "my bones," he handed her the paper. "Can you tell me what any of this means?"

She studied the page for a long time. "No idea at all." She turned it from side to side, as though a different angle might reveal its mystery.

"That's the last text message Mason sent me on my cell. Does that first part suggest anything to you?"

Amanda bit her lip doubtfully. In an instant, her eyes brightened with an idea. "If it's from Mason, it may refer to that." She gestured at the wall map of Washington. They went over and huddled before it. "He did love the District."

"Yes, I walked Washington with him whenever I came to town."

"He always described it as an imperfect diamond, flawed but still priceless. And when he'd write anything about the downtown area, he used a letter and number combination, because—I can hear him saying it, can't you?—that's the way it was designed. The Frenchman Pierre L'Enfant laid out the entire city like a giant grid, and an African American named Benjamin Banneker helped survey it. By naming streets with letters and numbers, it produced a shorthand for locating everything in town. N, of course, would be N Street, and it crosses 35th Street just about here." She placed a finger on the precise spot.

He inspected the map carefully. "That's the middle of Georgetown. Does that have any significance you can think of?"

"No." She sighed grimly. "But maybe that's not the right intersection after all. There'd be an N Street in Northeast D.C.," she added, pointing to the right on the map. "And one in Southeast Washington. And another here in Southwest. Do any of them mean anything to you?"

He solemnly shook his head. "Not a thing."

"He might have meant another city, but I doubt it. The District was always his obsession. I don't think he used the shorthand about anywhere else."

"Maybe Zelda can help us. She's a reporter downtown, and Mason was going to let her break our big story. He'd sent her an email."

Amanda's eyes suddenly lit up. "Then I'll bet she's I17."

"What are you talking about? Sounds like more bingo numbering, as Zelda suggested earlier."

Amanda returned to the computer and hit several buttons. "Look," she said, indicating "I17" in the subject line of a recent email. Pointing and clicking, she opened it to reveal the message Zelda had shown him earlier.

"I don't open Mason's emails usually," Amanda said, "but I did notice he was sending them out from wherever he was."

Klewe retraced his steps to the wall map. "If you're right, I17 must refer to the intersection of I Street and 17th."

"Not far from the White House in Northwest D.C. Does Zelda live around there?"

"I don't know." He leaned down to read the map's fine print at that intersection. "It says the Army-Navy Club. That's a club for military officers, isn't it?"

Amanda glanced back at the email on the screen. "And why did Mason decide to bring in a reporter? Did he sense how much danger he was in?"

Klewe, however, did not want her dwelling on that question. "What I could really use is the name of the person he was planning to see in Paris."

"I can't help with that. He never told me the guy's name."

"What about his trip plans? Did he leave an itinerary with you?"

"He faxed me a copy the other day. It's in my car."

As Amanda tugged open the front door, Zelda came from the kitchen with two steaming cups of tea. She was dressed again in her own clothes, clean and dried.

"I hope you like it strong," Zelda called out to her.

"My favorite way," she said, leaving the front door slightly ajar.

"Find anything?" Zelda handed a cup to Klewe, whose hands trembled slightly as he accepted it, and then placed the other atop a table near the couch.

"You aren't part of some secret military operation, are you?" he asked lightly.

"Not unless they're keeping it secret from me too. Why?"

"Amanda thinks Mason used letters and numbers as short-hand for downtown Washington. He labeled your email as I17, but that corner is Farragut Park and the Army-Navy Club." He indicated the spot on the map.

"Well, yes," Zelda said. "And it's The New York Times."

"What?"

"The Washington bureau for The Times. It's right there," she said, pointing at the same spot. "Inside the Army-Navy Club's building. The bureau has a separate entrance, but it's located upstairs there."

"According to these computer files, Mason sent one to you at 117 and another to somebody at L15."

Zelda glared at him petulantly. "Who was he talking to at The Post?"

"The Washington Post?"

"It's at L and 15th Streets Northwest. But I thought this story was supposed to be my exclusive. You never said you were involving other reporters."

"Hey, I didn't even involve you, remember? It was Mason."

"You're right." She held up her hands in surrender. "But if I'm going to be with you in the crossfire, I should have exclusive rights to it. I'll bet Amanda would back me up on that."

"No guarantees. I never thought it would put Mason's life in jeopardy, and I'm not in any hurry to put you in harm's way too."

She was starting to protest when he set down his cup forcefully and beckoned her back with his palm. His eyes widened in concern.

"In there," he said, almost inaudibly, motioning toward the bedroom as he tried to look through the glass slit in the front door.

"What? Where did Amanda go?"

"To her car. But she's been gone too long."

Klewe heard nothing outside as he moved stealthily toward the open cabin door. An instant before he could get there, though, the lights throughout the house flickered and went dark.

Chapter 16.

A CHILLING SILENCE permeated the inside of the cabin, infusing Klewe with a palpable sense of dread. He knew that, even if the front door were thrown wide open, there would be little illumination from outside for their escape past whoever was there. He also knew they needed time, and there was only one way to assure it.

"Be right there, Ammie," he called casually out the front door to the quiet night air. As he feared, there was no response from his friend. Without bothering to try the wall switch again, he closed the door from the inside and flipped the lock on the knob. There was no security bolt, as he knew from earlier visits to the cabin. Bumping into furniture as he crossed the polished floor, he worked his way to the far side of the room, stopping only long enough to lift his umbrella and Zelda's bag from a wall hook.

Zelda stood obscured in the unlit hallway to the back rooms. He took her arm and guided her to the kitchen area, where he had once helped Mason to close the windows against a fast-moving storm. Fumbling in the darkness now, he felt for the window above the sink and then fingered around its frame for the metal lock.

Klewe rapidly undid the lock and gave the window a quick thrust upward. It made a sharp scraping sound as it gave way. The opening would be small, but he hoped it was wide enough. With a gentle lift, he aided Zelda as she scrambled over the kitchen counter and through the window. Then he heard her drop gracelessly onto the ground outside. As he rolled over the counter himself, his forehead struck the top of the window frame, and he cursed to himself. From the next room, he could hear the sound of the front door being forced open.

Once outside the window, he regained his balance on the wet dirt and wordlessly nudged Zelda around the cabin toward the driveway. They moved clumsily through the brush, not daring to turn on the flashlight. The stale smell of wet leaves was heavy in the air around them. Beyond the cabin lay dense woods, and he considered heading toward the trees for cover, but he knew they would become an easy target there. Instead, he needed to locate Amanda and the car.

No lights had come on inside the cabin as they edged their way between the woods and the house. Traces of moonlight were still pushing their way through the clouds overhead. There was barely enough illumination to see the frame of Amanda's Dodge Charger, a red four-door parked across the lawn. In hurried uneven steps, they circled the outside of the cabin toward the car.

Zelda, making her way to the passenger side, paused when she thought she heard Klewe stumbling to the ground. "Chris?" Her whisper received no answer. Finally she heard him at the driver's side of the automobile.

"Get in," his voice came back in low sharp tones. "Now!"

Simultaneously they pulled open the car doors and slid inside. As they tried to shut the doors quietly, Klewe's arm scraped the steering wheel and sounded the car horn.

For an instant, the interior of the car remained lit up, scarcely long enough to cast a beam against the front of the cabin. In that second, they watched the door of the cabin come flying open, with a figure racing toward them in the night.

"Hold on!" Klewe inserted the ignition key and started the engine. With a grinding sound, the gearshift moved into position, and he stomped the gas pedal. Grudgingly, the car roared off across the lawn and away from the running shadow. He poked frantically at the headlight controls until high beams flooded the dirt road ahead. They swerved dangerously from side to side, picking up speed as the tires gained traction on the unpaved surface beneath them.

"Can you drive this thing?" Zelda asked, knowing as they lurched along that her question was too late to matter. The dashboard lights inside the Charger allowed her to spot a paper lying on the floor mat, and she bent down to retrieve it. "This could be Mason's travel plans," she said, unable to read the document clearly in the darkness.

Klewe made no comment. He kept his eyes staring soberly forward at the road ahead.

"Are you all right?" Again she received no response.

They were approaching the end of the long driveway, where the dirt lane would meet up again with Peachtree Road. Something stood ahead in their path, outlined in the car's streaming headlights. It was a yellow Vespa, Zelda noted, realizing the intruder must have left it there, approaching the cabin silently on foot from the motor scooter. She also noticed that the Charger was not slowing for the bike parked ahead of them in the road.

"Are you all right?" she asked again. "And where in the world did you find keys for this car?"

"On Amanda." He pushed his foot firmly against the accelerator as Zelda watched the car bearing resolutely down on the European scooter.

Chapter 17.

THE IMPACT OF the speeding sedan as it tore through its stationary target resulted in an ear-splitting crash. Pieces of the yellow Vespa went flying, its main frame upended off the side of the road.

After exhaling a deep breath, Klewe slowed the Dodge to a standstill and cautiously looked both ways for traffic on Peachtree before entering the roadway. They drove back into town without conversation until they came upon the lights of an all-night gas station. There on the corner stood an unused phone booth, and he swerved to a stop.

"I have to make a call."

"Where's your cell?"

He switched off the ignition. "Next to Amanda. I turned it on and dialed 911. With the GPS tracking, it should be easy enough for the police to find her." He sat there, hopelessly shaking his head.

"Listen to me, Chris. This is not your fault, none of it."

"Then," he asked in dolorously measured words, "exactly whose fault would it be?"

He climbed slowly out of the four-door and removed from his blazer pocket the card showing Detective Robinson's cell number, which he dialed. The gruff voice of the homicide detective made him realize how early in the morning the hour still was.

In staccato sentences, Klewe narrated the night's happenings, from the encounter with the security guard Hal Iger to Amanda's death. When he'd finished, Robinson ordered him to call the state police immediately. Klewe did not reply, and the detective took a harder line with him.

"Hang up the phone. I'll call the Maryland authorities right now. You need to get to my office as soon as you can drive there. Understand?"

"I'll try to."

"You do better than try. Meet me at the address on that card."

Klewe pocketed the card again and hesitated.

"Look," the detective added in a softer tone, "we'll figure all this out. But there's something else you need to know."

"What else?"

"It's about your girlfriend."

"What girlfriend?"

"Or whatever you call her. Mrs. Hart. I had some checking done. She's not a Times reporter. Hell, she's not even married. Klewe, did you hear me?"

By that time, however, the receiver was already replaced in its cradle, and Klewe shoved wide the door to the phone booth on his way out.

"What did Detective Robinson say?" Zelda watched him crawl back into the driver's seat of the Dodge.

"He wants us to drop by for more questioning."

"That's good, isn't it? We're going to need his help. What time does he want us there?"

"Not right away." He gunned the engine again. "I have an idea. Let's go by your office first at The Times."

Klewe and Zelda rode in silence for several moments as the Charger sped along the Maryland back roads toward the Washington Beltway. Eventually there was enough daylight suffusing the car that Zelda was able to read the page she'd found. She kept her eyes deliberately downcast, busily trying to interpret Mason Everly's itinerary.

"This isn't very useful," she finally announced.

"No help with his travel plans?"

"Uh-uh. Just a typed address and phone number for the hotel he was staying at in London. There's only one other notation. 'Shakespeare & Co.,' it says."

"That's a store in Paris."

"I already knew that." Klewe glanced sideways at her from the driver's seat. "No, I didn't. But I figured it wasn't a law firm."

Withholding a smile, he turned off the Beltway, and they headed along Canal Road into the District. Ahead in the distance stood the stark obelisk of the Washington Monument, growing taller as they traveled toward it.

The dawn traffic was gradually becoming more nettlesome during their ride, but in a few moments they were circling onto M Street at the edge of Georgetown.

"Why did you turn here?"

"I want to see what Mason may have meant by N35."

"Oh. I thought maybe you're a fan of 'The Exorcist.'" They were nearing a gas station, adjacent to which stretched the most famous outdoor stairway in the history of horror films. "That's where the Catholic priest took his long tumble, something like 75 stone steps down."

"I'm beginning to understand how he felt," Klewe said, steering Amanda's car onto M Street.

He waited for a red light to change and adjusted the headlights to low beams after an oncoming car flashed its lights at him. They cleared the corner where 35th intersects N Street, and he eased the car against the curb into a no-parking space.

With increasing disappointment, Klewe surveyed the restored townhouses and stores that lined the narrow streets. "I don't see anything here."

"Then you must not be into celebrity watching," Zelda responded, a touch of whimsy in her voice. "When John F. Kennedy was still a Senator and escorting Jacqueline about town, they attended that church over there. Actually, it's the oldest church in D.C., still in use after more than two centuries."

"A charming story, but I don't see its relevance."

"Did I promise relevance?"

He hunched forward to start the car up again. "Maybe you can show me around your office when we get there? And doesn't somebody get worried when you stay out all night? Maybe Mr. Hart?" It was his first mention of her marriage, and he deliberately failed to meet her gaze.

"I doubt the building is open yet," Zelda hedged, ignoring the other questions. "Besides, don't you owe me breakfast or something?"

"Something." He flipped the turn signal on and inched forward as he waited to pull away from the curb.

"You're always in such a hurry. If your friend Mason loved architecture, he must have known every building in this whole neighborhood."

"Maybe so."

"Look at the front of this one." She surveyed the exterior of the parish church the Kennedys had helped make famous. "I could imagine myself getting married here one of these days."

"Aren't you already married?"

"Of course not."

"Then what's with the ring?"

"Oh, this?" She waved the band of white gold indifferently. "Just a beard. Helps keep the losers away."

He felt a swift pang of relief, but was reluctant to admit it even to himself. "Then maybe you can get married here someday."

"Maybe." Zelda weighed the possibility. "But I don't think so. For one thing, I'm not Catholic. If I were, though, I sure wouldn't mind holding a big fancy wedding in Holy Trinity."

The car had been easing forward when Klewe slammed his foot down on the brake so hard that Zelda pitched forward and back in her seat. A passing truck swerved to avoid broadsiding the Charger where it now rested halfway into traffic. The truck driver blew the horn in disgust as he went by, while Klewe assiduously backed the car again toward the curb.

"Holy Trinity?" he repeated skeptically, killing the engine and leveling a disbelieving gaze at her. "Are you telling me this is Holy Trinity Church?"

Chapter 18.

KLEWE THREW THE gearshift into park while Zelda looked at him as though he'd gone mad. Solemnly she pointed at the sign afront the building. "Holy Trinity Church," he read aloud and let out a low whistle. "Thank you, Mason."

"Did your friend go to church here?"

"No. I mean, I don't know where Mason went to church. But when Shakespeare died, he was laid to rest in Stratford-upon-Avon in England's Holy Trinity Church."

"So you think Mason wanted to signal you about something in Stratford with N35?"

He nodded absentmindedly and proceeded to drive away from the curb. With a quick series of turns, they headed back into the heavier traffic of Georgetown.

Zelda began counting with her fingers. "The Kennedy church in Georgetown, the Kennedy Center on the Potomac. I'm beginning to detect an Oliver Stone pattern to your conspiracy theory. And what about 'my bones'?"

As he started to answer, a pair of drunken pedestrians plowed their way through a row of parked cars and stepped directly into their path. Again he had to stand on the brakes to stop in time. The jaywalkers, a middle-aged couple wearing the checkerboard costumes of harlequins with their faces painted half-black and half-white, laughed raucously at his efforts and slapped their hands onto the hood of the car. Then they crossed to the other side of the street and veered down a side alley.

"That was close," Zelda said.

"Too close. I know it's Halloween, but isn't it a little late for them to be out celebrating?"

"Or a little early."

"Let's go to The Times." He redirected the car onto M Street. "It's at 17th and I, you said?"

Zelda stared straight ahead at the Georgetown streets. "I keep trying to tell you. The building probably isn't open this early."

Klewe checked the clock on the car's dashboard. "It's almost seven now. If it's not open yet, it should be soon."

By now, the District roads were clogged with the morning commute into downtown Washington. From every direction, government and business employees streamed onto the sidewalks from commuter parking garages. Ahead of them in the road, an accordion Metrobus blocked their way, so they waited without speaking for the traffic to start moving again along Pennsylvania Avenue.

Zelda cracked open the passenger window and took in a deep breath of the smoggy morning air. Then she deliberately faced Klewe across the car seat.

"All right, I don't work for The New York Times. I mean, I do work for The Times, I'm just not ..." Again she stalled. "I'm not a reporter. There, I've said it."

"Not a reporter? Then why are you following me around?"

"I plan to be one sooner or later. It's just so hard to break into the field. I started to tell you I was only a stringer for them so far. I'm waiting to land a real story, not some fluff piece that doesn't go anywhere. So I took a part-time job with The Times when it came open. Not reporting, exactly, but I get to do some writing, if you can call it that. Among my responsibilities is helping keep the obituary files up to date about people who are still alive. Nobody knows when a leader or celebrity will die, and when it does happen, they'll have material they can rework from whatever I've started. It sounds morbid, but that's what I do. Satisfied?"

He relaxed his grip on the steering wheel. "I'm glad you finally told me. Detective Robinson had me wondering."

"What does he have to do with it?"

"When I called him, he told me you weren't married or a Times reporter. I was hoping you'd tell me the truth."

"Oh, I see. You were testing me?" Irately she twisted back in the passenger seat to face forward and fold her arms rigidly.

"You could say that." He flickered the turn signal and pulled off Pennsylvania Avenue. Before making the left, he noticed the road ahead of them was no longer open to traffic in front of the White House, one of the many long-term efforts to obstruct terrorist attacks in downtown D.C. Zelda, however, said nothing else, and he decided there was only one sure way to soften her anger. "I needed to be sure I can trust you with a big story."

Zelda's rage melted instantaneously into a crooked smile. "Then we should go to the bureau. There's somebody you have to meet."

They turned at the next corner for Farragut Park and started searching for an available parking space.

"By the way," she asked him beguilingly, "what do you want in your obit?"

Chapter 19.

THE CAR ANGLED into a metered space by Farragut Park, where the two began walking alongside a grassy promenade toward 17th Street. A flock of listless pigeons vied with them for sidewalk space. One pigeon took flight long enough to settle atop a statue of the Civil War hero David Farragut, the bird sitting astride the naval commander's head like a feathered top hat. Within their purview, commuters exited in large numbers onto the street level from the underground Metro stations at either end of the park.

Klewe grew more and more agitated, remembering their close calls of the night before, and began sounding unsure. "Maybe this isn't safe, going to your office."

"I write about dead people. How dangerous can it be?" Waiting on the park side of the intersection, she pointed out the Army-Navy Club in the building opposite them. They headed toward that structure's massive glass facade, but rather than going in there, Zelda led him around the corner and up a short stairway facing the cross street. Confidently she slid her electronic key into a slot and pulled the side door open. "This way to The Times."

A quick elevator ride carried them up several floors to a glassed-in landing where she again inserted her key into a wall slot. The heavy glass doors yielded easily. After presenting a quick tour of the open newsroom, she indicated a lengthy corridor that led to dozens of vacant cubicles for reporters and stretched past the fancier offices of Times columnists.

"This is where I'll work someday," she declared confidently before starting to descend a stairway in the middle of the newsroom. They reached the lower floor and stopped. "And down here is where I work now. It's not exactly an office. More like a space in back of the morgue—you know, the library. I don't know why it's called a morgue, but newspaper jargon does like to remind us of our own mortality. Do you know why reporters use the word 'deadlines'?" Klewe shook his head. "In the Civil War they drew lines around prison camps for captured enemy soldiers. If they stepped across the 'dead line,' as they called it, they were executed instantly."

Zelda led the way around another corner.

"Besides the morgue and the deadlines," she continued, relishing another chance to be the one lecturing, "we talk about burying the lead, we have graveyard editions and tombstone headlines and ghost writers, all kinds of gruesome imagery. Enough death to last a lifetime." She tossed a switch for overhead lights, and the entire length of the lower level was illuminated. Beyond the desks of the staff librarians stood her work station, little more than a table strewn with reference books and stacks of newspaper articles. "We rarely use clippings these days," she explained, almost apologetically. "The computer search systems are much faster than the old clip files. And now I'd like you to meet my secret weapon, someone who's even faster than the computers."

They turned down another hallway to see a bearded owlish man slouching over his desk. When Zelda called to the older man, he rose and slowly came to them, leaning heavily on a cane as he walked.

"Professor Christopher Klewe," she began, "this is Mr. James Harris, who is quite simply the world's best researcher. James can find out everything about everything for you." The jovial man's eyes twinkled at the compliment as he put down the cane to extend his hand.

"The Shakespeare scholar?" Harris asked her with delight, and Zelda nodded enthusiastically. "This is a real pleasure for me, Professor."

"I've been hearing good things about you too."

"Ah, Ms. Hart is too kind." The researcher clasped his hands together. "I know your work on the Bard well. If I can ever be of assistance, just ask."

"We were hoping," Zelda said, "you could tell us something about the term 'white crow.'" As soon as she'd said the words, Klewe shot her an angry look, but she gestured for him not to worry.

"White crow? I'll look into it." Harris pointed over to Zelda's work station. "Meanwhile, I wanted to let you know I'd found a delivery for you on the front steps this morning. I put it there by your in-box."

Zelda thanked him and watched as Harris lifted the cane and headed back to his desk. Then she checked her work station and began to open a small cardboard box, momentarily struggling with its wrapping paper. "What in the world is this?" Suddenly the blood drained from her face.

"What's the matter?"

"It says it's from Mason," she said, dropping the package onto the table.

"His flash drive?" Klewe asked hopefully, reaching for the box.

"No. His ear."

Chapter 20.

WITH A RIGID arm, Klewe stiffly pushed Zelda back a few steps from the table and stared down into the partially opened package. Inside was a small dark mass embedded with something shiny. Nausea began to overcome him when he recognized the gold stud as Mason Everly's earring still protruding from flesh.

"What kind of person could do that? And why send it to me?" Her questions went unanswered while Klewe was intently examining the box and its contents. The outside of the package did show his colleague's name printed as the sender, but there was nothing handwritten within, merely a page torn from a book of Shakespeare's poems.

"It's a copy of Sonnet 55," he said, unfolding the bloodied page that had served as a wrapper. Then he produced a handkerchief from his jacket pocket and used it to repackage the contents of the small box. On a larger envelope he found at Zelda's desk, he scribbled a name and address, then carefully placed the box inside and sealed it.

When he asked Zelda the best way to have it sent to Detective Robinson, she reached apprehensively for the package. "I'll be right back," she said, rushing up the stairs to arrange the delivery. By the time she returned a few moments later, she found Klewe sitting at her work station and formulating a plan.

"We need to get out of here." He stood up when he saw her. "Do you have your passport with you?"

"Yes, but why? Do we need it for Detective Robinson?"

"No, for Europe."

"I thought you were told not to go far."

He forced a grin. "'Far' is such a relative term."

"I'll buy that," she said, leaning down to unlock a small drawer in the metal cabinet by her table. "I keep my passport here at work. But what about clothes? Can I at least go home to pack some things?"

He took Zelda by the hand. "You can't go home now. We can't even go to my Jeep in the Folger lot. We can't take that kind of chance." Her eyes questioned him about the urgency. "Don't you see? They obviously know who you are. And they know where you are."

Although she seemed dubious about their unplanned travel, Klewe remained resolute in getting her to reconsider.

"Hold on a minute, Zelda, and think this through. They know you're with me, which makes you part of all this. Are you sure getting a big story will be worth it?"

She did not answer him directly, because she was already sweeping a handful of items off the desktop into her Coach bag. They headed for a side exit, but not until after she stopped to inform James Harris of her immediate need to take some leave. He promised to pass the word along and handed her a page from his printer.

"Take this along," he said. "Nothing recent about a white crow, but I found a little something you might want to know."

Zelda thanked him, placing the paper unread into her shoulder bag.

"Be safe," Harris told her, lifting a hand to wave farewell at Klewe, "the two of you." When the older man called out to him protectively, "She's the best," Klewe waved back agreeably.

They rode the elevator down to the lobby where Zelda asked, "How about getting something to eat?"

"Breakfast at the airport," he offered, checking his pocket watch. "Or lunch maybe."

"I'll have both." She patted her stomach as they walked back to their parking space adjacent to Farragut Park. "I guess we don't have time to do anything else." She grabbed the keys to Amanda's car from his hand. "But this time I'll drive."

"Hey, cut me a little slack," Klewe complained lightly. "I drive stick." He took the passenger seat in the red Charger while Zelda started the car and directed it haphazardly into traffic. After she made a left turn onto Pennsylvania Avenue, he commented, "We're going the wrong way for the airport."

Spinning the wheel effortlessly, she executed a perfect U-turn in the middle of one of downtown Washington's busiest streets. "Better?" she asked.

Klewe didn't answer until after he reopened his eyes. By then, they were traveling rapidly back toward Georgetown, and neither one noticed that a black Cadillac Escalade had made an identical U-turn on Pennsylvania Avenue immediately behind them.

Chapter 21.

"I WANT TO hear what else Shakespeare said," Zelda insisted as her hands performed a constant drum roll on the steering wheel. "Did he write much about prejudice?"

Klewe tried not to watch the road as they sped across the Potomac on Key Bridge and swerved onto the George Washington Memorial Parkway in Virginia. "A whole lot more than most of the writers in his time. You have to remember, though, that even back then racial difference was a sensitive topic. And he was writing for an audience that had some strong preconceived notions. If they ever celebrated blackness, it was probably in old folksongs about the color of their true love's hair."

"So what did Shakespeare write?"

"He tried to develop his audience's sense of humanity and awareness of the growing world around them. On the night that Romeo first sees Juliet, for example, Romeo describes her beauty 'as a rich jewel in an Ethiop's ear.' Shakespeare had no reason to make a reference to somebody African at that moment, but he worked it in anyway. He also wrote some telling passages about tolerance in 'The Merchant of Venice,' if you know that play."

"I liked it a lot when I saw it in college."

"Then you may remember that the Jewish character of Shylock is treated as the outsider in the play, usually painted as a villain. But Shakespeare is never that shallow in his treatment of characters. Shylock gives a memorable speech pointing out society's unfair treatment of Jews. 'I am a Jew,' he says. 'Hath not a Jew eyes? Hath not a Jew hands?' Then he asks, 'If you prick us, do we not bleed? If you tickle us, do we not laugh? If you poison us, do we not die?'"

"I get it. Everybody's human." She honked the horn at a slow-moving pickup ahead of them.

"That's right. Then there's even more discrimination displayed in that comedy when a black character enters. The Prince of Morocco."

"He's tries to woo the leading lady, doesn't he?"

"Yes. Portia is an unmarried heiress, whose late father set up a contest. She's courted by men who have to choose between caskets of gold, silver and lead. If they choose correctly, they win her hand in marriage."

"If they're wrong, though, didn't they have to accept a terrible fate?"

"They have to agree they will forever remain unmarried."

"Some punishment," she said sarcastically. "As I recall, though, the Prince chooses the wrong box."

"And loses the contest. Of course, if you read the play carefully, Portia cheats in favor of the winner, the white man that she wants to marry. Meanwhile, the Prince makes some extraordinary comments about being black in a predominantly white society. He tries to gain Portia's affections in his very first words by saying, 'Mislike me not for my complexion.' He tells her, 'I would not change this hue except to steal your thoughts.' He's proud of his heritage, while Portia clearly shows her deep prejudice against people of color. After the Prince leaves, she says, 'Let all of his complexion choose me so.' It's the same kind of prejudice Othello faces from his white father-in-law, who assumes it must be drugs or witchcraft that made his white daughter fall in love with a black man."

Zelda pushed down harder on the gas pedal to overtake other cars on the parkway. "Sounds like Shakespeare was probably trying to make his audience take a look at their own prejudices."

"I think you're right," Klewe said, "but you may want to slow down a little. We're not in that big a hurry."

"Then stop closing your eyes, and let go of the dash. So what else did Shakespeare say on the subject?"

"Oh, you can find plenty of anti-black references in his writings too. Mostly the kind of cultural notions that his audience would buy into without thinking twice about the subject. What stands out, though, are the other places that he writes in favor of blackness, something his contemporaries were probably surprised by, maybe even outraged about. He repeatedly compliments the beauty of black eyes and black hair and black complexion in a society that preferred fair features."

"That must have made him seem out of place," Zelda said, taking a long glance in the rearview mirror. "What the hell's wrong with this guy behind us?"

Klewe cast a look at the outside mirror to see a raven Escalade gaining ground in back of them. "Doesn't he think you're going fast enough?"

"I can't tell what his problem is. Anyway, was Shakespeare making observations like that in his poems as well or just his plays?"

"Both, really. In a play like 'The Two Gentlemen of Verona,' he emphasizes a saying that 'Black men are pearls in beauteous ladies' eyes.' Then in one of his sonnets, he explains that times are changing because 'In the old age black was not counted fair,' but he says black is becoming 'beauty's successive heir.' He's even more blunt in a later sonnet where he vows, 'Thy black is fairest in my judgment's place.'"

"Those must have been shocking words back then." She picked up her speed again, but as she did, they felt a sudden jolt as the Charger was bumped from the back. "Son of a bitch!" Zelda shouted, frantically adjusting the rearview mirror. "It's that SUV again!"

"I can't even see who's driving," Klewe said, trying his best to turn in the passenger seat to catch a view of the other vehicle. "His windows are tinted too dark. Should we stop?"

"I've got this," she assured him and pressed down again on the accelerator.

A second bump followed, and then a third, this time hard enough to spill the contents from Zelda's bag onto the Dodge's floormat.

"We're almost to the Beltway. I can definitely shake him there."

Zelda pulled forward again, the speedometer rising to its highest number so far. They passed the sign for a Capital Beltway turnoff, and Zelda made a sharp turn onto the 495 without signaling. Just behind them, the Cadillac made the same turn.

She punched the gas pedal and slid the car across three lanes of busy traffic, but the Escalade stayed right with them. "Hold on," she advised Klewe needlessly as they quickly shot past an arrow pointing them toward Dulles Airport.

"Shouldn't we pull off?" Klewe suggested to her again, but Zelda was not yielding her eyes from the fast-advancing roadway. "Maybe get some help."

"Not yet," she said, making the sharp right onto the Dulles access road. Again the black vehicle followed in close succession. "Not just yet."

They passed a series of road construction warnings, but there was no work crew visible on the scene. Ahead, though, was a distant overpass where a lone vehicle sat idling. As they got closer, Klewe could make out the markings of the Virginia Highway

Patrol. Near the car a state trooper was standing and pointing a radar gun in their direction.

Zelda steered wildly off the highway, kicking up dust and gravel along the shoulder as she stomped hard on the Charger's brake. They came to a squealing stop only a few feet behind the trooper's car. Then they watched as the black SUV slowed down but continued on by them, disappearing over a ridge ahead.

With a contrite smile, Zelda waved timorously at the trooper, who shook his head disapprovingly of her stop on the shoulder and gestured for her to move along. She checked the rearview mirror and signaled to come carefully back onto the road surface.

"Is he gone?" Klewe wondered, staring off into the distance for the raven Cadillac.

"He'd better be. He doesn't know what kind of new one I was planning to rip him when we stopped."

"We'll be at Dulles soon. That should be safe enough."

Noticing his knuckles had turned white against the dashboard, Zelda asked lightly, "So how do you like my driving now?"

"It makes me think we're already in Paris."

"Paris? I thought you said your talk was in London."

He gave up searching for the Cadillac along the access road and studied the upcoming signs for airport parking. "You're the one who found Mason's itinerary, and it mentioned Paris, so that's our first stop."

"No," she corrected him. "Our first stop will be much sooner than that."

THE THIRD ACT:
RACE OF HEAVEN

Chapter 22.

"GUM?" KLEWE PRETENDED to grumble at an oblivious Zelda inside the passenger lounge of Dulles International Airport. "That's what you made us stop for?"

"Helps pop my ears at takeoff," she explained nonchalantly.

Dulles itself, located in a Northern Virginia suburb less than an hour's drive from downtown D.C., proved as noisy and crowded as they'd expected, with the usual bustle of travelers frantic to make their scheduled departures. When Klewe returned from buying a newspaper, he surveyed the mound of candy wrappers and emptied snack food containers around Zelda. From her hand dangled a paperback, which she had stopped reading to daydream out a dusty airport window.

He tapped her shoulder and indicated the book she held listlessly. "Not 'The Da Vinci Code,' I take it."

"More like 'Da Vinci Codeine.'" She made an effort to rouse herself and dropped the novel on the next chair over.

"Sure you don't want more to eat?" he asked facetiously. She ignored the tone.

"No, breakfast and lunch helped. How much longer till the flight, though? Maybe they'll serve something."

"Not much longer." He saw the impatience in her expression. "We showed up here without a reservation and changed my London flight tomorrow to two seats for Paris today, so I think we're pretty lucky to be going anywhere."

"You're probably right. At least we're done with that security checkpoint. Not even the School of Night would want to follow us through that."

Klewe considered her words. "I doubt whoever's chasing us would bring a weapon in here. But in the meanwhile," his expression grew stern, "there's still a little matter of truthfulness to discuss."

"What?" she asked innocently. "I've admitted I lied to you about who I am and what I do, as well as my marital status. Oh, and my hair is naturally auburn instead of blond. That about covers it, don't you think?"

"Not quite." He removed the glass-covered clover from his shirt pocket and placed the ornament in her hand. "Why did you lie about this?"

"I didn't. That was a gift for you."

"From Shakespeare's grave?"

"Uh-huh."

"If you're going to lie, at least make it a good one. Like that ring you wear. People can get the wrong idea."

"Oh," she said, pulling the white-gold ring off her finger. "I guess it's time I lost this thing. At least I won't be needing it around you."

"What's that supposed to mean?"

She bit her lip as she thought. "You're not my type. Too work-oriented. I bet you're the type who will make notes for your next class while we're traveling." When he failed to deny it, she laughed out loud. "I knew it. Have you ever been married?"

He grew reticent. "Almost," he finally said. "Things didn't work out."

"I'm sorry." Zelda displayed the ring ostentatiously before him, but her eyes held no sentiment. "I was married once. For about a minute. He left, so I held onto the ring." She deposited the jewelry into her shoulder bag, which she pushed aside on the seat. Having palmed the clover in her other hand, she produced it to return to him. "So how could you tell I was lying about this?"

"Too easy. Shakespeare's tomb is inside Holy Trinity Church. There is no grave. No place to pick clover or anything else. Where did you get this?"

"So much for Internet bargains. Well, at least they let him be buried in the church. That's better than how the Fitzgeralds were treated."

"Well, to be fair, Shakespeare's Holy Trinity wasn't Catholic."

"But I take it he was considered an important person in Stratford."

"Yes, at least after he retired. But there are all kinds of ugly stories about why he left Stratford in the first place. That he abandoned his wife, leaving her to rear three small children by herself. That he was arrested for poaching and forced to leave town. That he was a deadbeat dad and made his living in various unsavory ways as a young man. In fact, scholars call that lost time his 'dark years.'" They exchanged a wry smile. "By the time he came back to retire in Stratford, though, he was a wealthy man. There are records of the house he bought and the properties he owned."

"What about his relationship with his family?"

"That's another question. We don't know how he got along with his father, for instance, but he did manage to acquire something his father always wanted and was never able to get. A coat of arms for the Shakespeares. Back then it was a real point of honor to have one, turning a common man into a gentleman, but his father kept being turned down. Finally, William succeeded in getting it for him. A family coat of arms, with the crest showing a falcon with a spear in its talon."

"Did getting it make his father proud of him?"

"Can't say. William was the eldest son in a family of eight children. And he did choose London over the family business in Stratford. My guess would be that his father was not exactly thrilled with him or his career choices back in those days."

A booming loudspeaker summoned them to the gate for their departing flight. Klewe scooped up his umbrella where it rested against a wall and aimed her toward the line of boarding passengers.

"Did that ever change?" Zelda asked, flipping the paperback into her bag and gathering the empty food wrappers to toss out.

"Eventually he made more money than his father had ever imagined and could afford that elusive coat of arms for their family. If that isn't enough to make a father proud—"

"I wouldn't know," she sighed wistfully. They handed their tickets to the gate attendant after a brief wait in line.

"I think his father must have made peace with him by then. Of course, there may have been a real sticking point in their relationship."

"What's that?"

Klewe motioned her to step ahead of him onto the Air France jet. "Whether his father was his father."

Chapter 23.

"I SEE WHAT you're saying." Zelda led the way as they side-stepped other travelers and settled into close-quarter seats for the international flight. "You're saying it was Shakespeare's mother who cheated. An interracial affair."

Klewe rubbed his scalp roughly. "Or his father may have had the affair, then asked his wife to take in the child. No one can say for certain what happened in the Shakespeare family, but there are precedents in the history of Great Britain. Scotland's royal blood-lines, for example, are said to include ancient references to black kings, and black babies were not unheard of in the British Isles."

"What about in England itself?"

"Mason found medieval reports of babies being born there with dark skin, but they were often subjected to vicious abuse, at-tacked as products of witchcraft. By the time of Shakespeare's par-ents, though, there were considerable numbers of African men and women who had traveled to England. Sure, they might have been a rare sight in the English countryside, but not an impossibility. And who's able to say with any certainty in the days before blood tests whether anybody's parents were their biological parents?"

"Paternity tests are big business today," she acknowledged, "but I doubt there was any way to know for sure back then. Except for the obvious."

"From family resemblance and skin color, you mean. As you said before, even if Shakespeare was biracial, that doesn't mean his skin was necessarily dark. These days we have TV talk shows discussing prejudice, and they often feature people who pass for members of another race despite their racial makeup."

"That's what you think Shakespeare did?"

"I think it may have been obvious enough that others would have noticed and probably tried to use it against him. If there's one topic he used in play after play, it was the question of a child's parentage. In 'King Lear,' for example, the Earl of Gloucester's first son is legitimate, but his second is a bastard named Edmund, who betrays his father in every possible way. Paternity issues cause a lot of controversy in Shakespeare."

Zelda recalled, "I remember there was a firestorm several years ago at the news that Thomas Jefferson had an interracial relationship with Sally Hemings leading to a number of children. Since that time, though, I've read that Jefferson's black descendants and white descendants have come together for family reunions."

"As it should be. It's only skin color, and that shouldn't matter. Besides, we can't say for certain that Mary Shakespeare did 'cheat,' for want of a better word, on her husband. By the time William was conceived, though, Mary was a young Catholic woman who had already given birth to two daughters, and we know one of them died in infancy, maybe both. That would be an awful lot of grief and guilt for anybody to handle."

"That's true."

"Think about 'Othello.' That play's entire premise rests on how the white Desdemona cannot help but be drawn to her dark-skinned husband. If Mary met someone and it didn't work out, perhaps John Shakespeare agreed to raise the child as his own. She had five more children after William and stayed married to John until he died. Maybe he never knew the truth, or maybe he always knew the truth. Perhaps he accepted William as his son and at the same time resented him. That could certainly cause a deep father-child rift, which is another theme Shakespeare used a lot."

"I don't suppose people were much more faithful to their spouses in those days, were they?"

"Not really. They say that Shakespeare's first child, Susannah, was accused of adultery after she got married."

Halfway listening to the flight attendant's speech on safety procedures, Zelda unwrapped several pieces of gum and began chewing energetically for takeoff.

The Air France jet roared ahead and lifted up from the runway. After several minutes, an announcement allowed passengers to loosen their seatbelts. Zelda moved closer to see what paperback Klewe had removed from his blazer pocket. It was a collection of Shakespeare's sonnets. "Ever read these?" he asked.

"In college. But I never got much out of them. You carry them with you?"

"I might need them in case of a Shakespeare emergency." He grinned sheepishly at her and thumbed indiscriminately through the pages. "Here's one everybody knows. It begins, 'Shall I compare thee to a summer's day? Thou art more lovely and more temperate.'"

As Klewe read aloud the rest of Sonnet 18, Zelda sat back in her seat, mesmerized by the words.

"'So long as men can breathe or eyes can see,'" he concluded, "'So long lives this, and this gives life to thee.'"

"Take me here, take me now," she begged him playfully. "Actually, I don't think I could explain a single word you just read, but you had me at 'lovely.'"

"Well, don't get too carried away. Shakespeare wrote that to another man."

She laughed. "Now that would be my luck."

"How about this?" He turned to a later page. "I want you to read Sonnet 55 for yourself."

When Zelda gave a tiny shiver, Klewe remembered it was the same sonnet she'd found in the bloodied office delivery. He started to take back the book, but she looked through the volume for the appropriate page and sighed heavily, obviously thinking it was going to be a long flight.

"'Not marble nor the gilded monuments of princes,'" she read aloud and stopped until Klewe motioned her to continue. She started over and slowly made her way through all 14 lines of Sonnet 55:

> Not marble nor the gilded monuments
> Of princes shall outlive this pow'rful rhyme,
> But you shall shine more bright in these contents
> Than unswept stone, besmeared with sluttish time.
> When wasteful war shall statues overturn,
> And broils root out the work of masonry,
> Nor Mars his sword, nor war's quick fire, shall burn
> The living record of your memory.
> 'Gainst death and all oblivious enmity
> Shall you pace forth; your praise shall still find room
> Even in the eyes of all posterity
> That wear this world out to the ending doom.
> So till the judgment that yourself arise,
> You live in this, and dwell in lovers' eyes.

When she came to the poem's conclusion, she scanned the printed words again. Then she closed the book and handed it back to him.

"What does that say to you?" he prompted her.

"That I wasn't in college long enough."

"Come on. 'You live in this, and dwell in lovers' eyes.' What do you think it sounds like?"

"It sounds a little bit like the one you read before. The poem will outlast the person who's being written about, so that person will live on in its words."

"Bravo! That's exactly it. The poem will survive us all. And when you want to hide a secret, something that's meant to be found a long time after you're gone, what better place to hide it?"

"Than in a poem. And you say there's something hidden in Sonnet 55?"

"Yes. What do you know about the number 55?"

She grew thoughtful. "I know it's the speed limit we broke today, and traffic cops sometimes call it 'double nickels' because of its two fives. Let me see. I think it's also supposed to be the emerald anniversary. And when I worked as a waitress years ago, it was the slang order for root beer. What else?"

"It's in the Fibonacci number sequence."

"Wasn't that the one Dan Brown wrote about?"

"Right, where each number is the sum of the two numbers before it. Start with 0, 1, then another 1, 2, 3, 5 and 8." He slowed to make sure his math was correct. "Then 13, 21 and 34. The next number after that will be 55, which also happens to be the exact sum of all the numbers up to 10."

"Sounds about right," she said hesitantly after some figuring on her fingers.

"Also, when dice players roll the same number on each die, such as the two fives in 55, they call that a doublet."

"I thought a doublet was something men used to wear back in olden times."

"It was, but now it's also a dice term for two fives or two of whatever number."

Zelda's eyes lit up. "Which makes Barack Obama a doublet, doesn't it? He's our 44th President. And he's biracial." She directed her attention back to the sonnet collection. "But what makes 55 so special in Shakespeare's work?"

"Think this through. It's the poem numbered 55 in a collection of 154 sonnets. Some scholars claim that Shakespeare had nothing to do with the order of his sonnets, that the numbering is arbitrary. But the placement of this particular sonnet is just too perfect for me to believe it. What would you consider special about the number 55 in a group of 154?"

"It's not the exact middle." She did a quick mental calculation. "It's not even the start of the second third."

"But it does start something."

She gave him an uncertain look before starting to get his implication. "The last 100. It's the start of the last 100."

"Yes. It's not just some random number. And this one is also one of his most popular sonnets. The perfect place for a secret message."

By now Zelda's attention was hooked. "A secret message?" Insistently she opened the book of sonnets he was holding. "Show me."

Chapter 24.

KLEWE WRESTED A pen from his pocket and flattened out the collection of sonnets atop the tray table before him. "One way to make an anagram," he explained, "is to scramble the first letters of a poem's head words. Are you familiar with what head words are?"

Zelda raised her eyes pensively. "I don't think so."

"Those are the first words of each line in a poem. Here." He made a list down the inside of the book cover. "These are all the head words from Sonnet 55." He showed her the completed list:

Not
Of
But
Than
When
And
Nor
The
'Gainst
Shall

Even

That

So

You

Zelda counted the 14 head words from the sonnet. Then he pulled the book closer to designate a second list.

"Anagrams use a set pattern, such as the first letter of each line. The finished anagram should be able to account for every letter in that pattern. Most sonnets, for instance, are 14 lines long. To find the anagram in Sonnet 55, you take the first letter from each line."

In a column next to the head words, he quickly prepared a list of their initial letters:

N

O

B

T

W

A

N

T

'G

S

E

T

S

Y

Once that process was completed, he counted to make sure he had a full list of the 14 letters.

"There, that's all of them. You'll notice the letter used most often is T, which occurs three times. Each T forms a cross, so it can separate two parts. Here the T appears three times, indicating there will be four parts altogether."

"But what's being separated into four parts?"

"Let's look at the letters that are left." He used the pen again to cross out each T, leaving the following 11 letters:

N
O
B
W
A
N
'G
S
E
S
Y

"I don't see anything there." She kept studying the list. "How about giving me a little hint?"

"Okay," he said, "the term 'upstart crow' was meant to be an insult, but there's another common bird term used for Shakespeare."

She stopped to consider. "I've heard people refer to him sometimes as a swan. The Swan of Avon, right?"

"Good. So let's take the letters for 'swan' out of the list." He crossed off four more letters, leaving a total of seven:

N
O
B

'G

E

S

Y

When he finished, he handed her the pen. "And now here's where I started to get very intrigued by this sonnet. If you look carefully, you'll see a common term for 'black' in the list."

"Ebony!" she exclaimed, her excitement rising. Giving his hand a powerful squeeze, she added, "I told you I was good at Scrabble."

"I believe it." He waited as she removed five more letters from the list.

Zelda frowned at what remained. "It's a G and an S."

"That's the one hitch. It would have been perfect, of course, if it had left W and S as Shakespeare's initials."

"Well, what do G and S stand for?"

"Mason and I had been working on that. In fact, it's the main problem we were hoping to solve before announcing our theory."

"Maybe somebody else in the Shakespeare family had G as their first initial."

"We thought about that. There was, in fact, a Shakespeare sibling whose first name started with G. One of William's younger brothers was named Gilbert. But there would be no reason for Shakespeare to encode a message about Gilbert, at least not one we could think of."

She stared at the list of letters. "Then I don't see how you can say this anagram refers to William Shakespeare."

"I was hoping Mason had discovered something in London. Look again at the letters, though. See what else is unusual about that G?"

She pondered the list some more. "The apostrophe," she said a moment later. "It's the only letter that has an apostrophe in front of it."

"Precisely. Shakespeare could have used 'from' or any word he wanted to begin that line. He chose to use 'Against.' But then again he didn't use 'Against,' at least not exactly."

"Because that would be two syllables and throw off the rhythm of the line."

"That's just it. He used the contraction "Gainst' so that an apostrophe would replace the letter A at the beginning. That makes it a marked G, and I'm certain he was marking it to get our attention." He shut his eyes resignedly. "I just don't know why. Maybe because William was born before Gilbert?"

"You've had almost no sleep for two days," Zelda said to him. "Relax and rest your eyes awhile. You can tell me more when we get to Paris. Like where we'll be heading once we're there."

"You already told me, remember?" Keeping both eyes closed, he arched an eyebrow at her. "Shakespeare and Company."

Chapter 25.

AMID THE NEXT morning's turmoil inside Charles de Gaulle Airport, Zelda was alone, waiting for Klewe to come back with French euros.

She watched while scores of people hurried beside the row of airport chairs where she'd chosen to sit. A female traveler from India stopped to quiet an unhappy infant, and the two women exchanged patient smiles after Zelda waved at the baby. When the woman's husband arrived to rush them along, she noted he was a short Hispanic man with a mustache. The frenzied parents gathered up the child along with the mounds of paraphernalia needed for traveling with an infant, and the entire family vanished down a corridor toward a distant ticketing area.

At that moment Klewe reappeared in the flow of the crowd, and she beckoned for him to take the adjacent seat.

"Don't ever exchange money in an airport," he said with disgust as he put away his credit card, then lightened his tone. "Everything all right?"

She gave him a puzzled frown. "I've been sitting here watching all the people in this airport. There have been dozens of interracial couples, something I normally wouldn't notice. They're everywhere around Washington, but I guess I've never stopped to consider the difficulties they must have to face from their families and their communities."

"I know, and something like 10 percent of Americans are in interracial marriages, according to the statistics I've seen. It's hard nowadays to believe it was ever unacceptable, but think how it would have stood out in Renaissance England."

"When I was little, I'd read about Pocahontas and how she married an Englishman and went to London with him. How in the world could she have ever made that adjustment?"

"I can't imagine being a Native American in Shakespeare's London. That was some of the research Mason was doing. There are British public records from that time demonstrating how free black people not only lived in London then, but they also intermarried with white citizens, in mixed marriages that were legally recognized."

"Back in the days poets were being called crows and swans. How odd to think of people in bird terms."

"It's a tradition that actually goes back for centuries. Long before Ben Jonson referred to Shakespeare as 'Sweet Swan of Avon' in the First Folio, using that bird for a poet was a common classical allusion. The Latin poet Virgil, for instance, was the 'Swan of Mantua.' And in Greek myth, Zeus turned himself into a swan to impregnate the mortal Leda, who later gave birth to Helen of Troy. I guess being thought of as a swan made the poet seem godlike."

"I have to wonder, though, what Shakespeare's wife thought of all this."

"That's a lot harder to gauge," Klewe admitted. "Anne Hathaway is the great silent figure in all of literary history. I've often wondered what her reaction was to her husband's career when he moved 100 miles away from Stratford to the heady world of lower London. She may in fact have been the biggest supporter of his career, but unfortunately some people make her out to be the shrew he left town to get away from."

"Why do you think that is?"

"Who knows? They married when he was only 18 and she was already 26. Not only was she eight years older, but it may have been a shotgun wedding, because their daughter Susannah was born soon afterward. Anne eventually outlived her husband by seven years, but she passed away just months before the First Folio was released. We'll never know if she approved of the Folio or that engraving of Shakespeare on the title page."

"Sounds to me like they waited for her to die before they released it. Maybe she didn't want a false picture of her husband to go into print."

"I've wondered about that too." He got to his feet and searched the signs posted overhead for the fastest way to exit the airport.

"Where are we going now?"

"To find the cab line. We won't be in Paris very long, and we don't want to spend a week finding our way into town, do we?"

She strapped her bag over her shoulder as he elbowed their way into the constant stream of travelers. "Oh, I wouldn't mind a week in Paris," she replied, almost too lightly for him to hear.

The terminal doors opened underneath giant "Sortie" signs, and the two of them walked outside to find a clear sunny morning.

"Ever been to Paris?"

Zelda shook her head. "I did locate a city map in the airport lounge while I was waiting for you." She started digging to the bottom of the Coach bag. At length she drew out a folded paper and opened it to read.

"I take it you found the map."

"Something even better," she said. "It's that page of research James Harris gave me before we left The Times bureau. But one thing has been bothering me."

"Only one? Tell me."

"I know we're being chased by someone, but you've said there's an entire School of Night." Zelda looked around nervously at each person in the taxi line. "What if this someone who's after us turns out to be many more than one someone?"

Chapter 26.

"YOU'RE RIGHT TO worry about the number we're facing," Klewe said. "That's what a conspiracy is. The word means 'to breathe together,' usually in planning some evil plot." As they climbed into a cab, he added quickly, "Let's hope there aren't too many."

The vehicle pulled away from the curb while Zelda stayed immersed in the research she was reading.

"You're missing all the sights," Klewe remonstrated repeatedly as the airport taxi made its 15-mile journey into the heart of Paris. He had already interrupted her reading once to extol the beauty of the Eiffel Tower in the distance. Soon they would arrive in the middle of town, passing near the glass pyramid of the Louvre and the resplendent exterior of Notre Dame.

Zelda offered a single wave of her fingers and kept studying the page from James Harris spread out in front of her.

For a few moments Klewe sat back and relaxed. He did not really mind taking a circuitous route to wind past the sights of his favorite French city. Perhaps, he thought, they might find time to see the carefully guarded Mona Lisa. Then he recalled the long hot wait in the tourist lines and thought better of the idea.

"So what has the world's best researcher found for us?"

Zelda reread the paper. "Nothing about 'white crow' from any modern-day conspiracy, but he did find something interesting in British history. Have you ever heard of someone named Stephen Gosson?"

Klewe reflected. "There was a Renaissance writer by that name, an older man who was a contemporary of Shakespeare. What about him?"

"According to what James found for us, Gosson wrote some pretty nasty comments about the evils of the London theater back in those days."

"That's right. If I remember correctly, he wrote about the sinfulness of going to plays. Of course, he'd written some plays himself, so he wasn't the perfect person to cast stones. What about him?"

"I think Gosson may have been the one who helped name our nemesis. He wrote that people who were chaste or being properly religious would not want to be caught dead in the vicinity of London's playhouses. Finding good people in those places, he said, was as rare as seeing 'a black swan, and a white crow.'"

"Really?" Klewe excitedly took the notes from her. "Those exact words?"

"Told you James was the best."

"I shouldn't have doubted you."

As he perused the page, Zelda turned her attention to the sights outside. Klewe finished reading and folded up the research. When he tucked the paper into his blazer pocket, he found the itinerary from Amanda's car, which they'd abandoned in a long-term parking space at Dulles. He opened the travel print-out, but it revealed merely a cancelled reservation at a London hotel, followed by the insertion of "Shakespeare and Co." that Zelda had seen.

Their taxi crossed the Paris bridge onto the famed Left Bank. Zelda, staring over at the Seine River, tried to follow up on an earlier question without looking at him. "Did you ever forgive your brother? For pushing you into the river?"

"Never had the chance," Klewe said sadly but honestly. "Jackson drowned trying to save me."

She was dumbstruck by the answer. "Chris, I'm so sorry," she finally managed, truly remorseful. "I shouldn't have pried." Klewe said nothing more, and she patted his arm consolingly.

Sudden quick turns from one street to another began to propel them back and forth inside the taxi. Trying to shield Zelda from the turbulence, Klewe worried the cab driver had somehow been offended by them or misunderstood the fractured French of his directions. After a precarious swerve toward a low curb, the seemingly irate driver brought the cab to a dizzying halt between two Smart cars.

Zelda staggered out onto the Paris thoroughfare first, while Klewe tried in basic French to debate the exorbitant fare being demanded. When he realized the futility of arguing, he paid the driver. Then he lifted his umbrella and slipped out of the taxi seat onto a wide sidewalk.

He stood and marveled at the English wording on the store ahead of them, here in the midst of a city that frowned heavily upon anything not French. Zelda was spinning about, her eyes wide to take in the views of every direction. Klewe stepped past her on the sidewalk to reach for a doorknob and ushered her inside the green front of the building at 37 rue de la Bucherie.

"Good," he declared, "they opened at 10." He made a triumphal gesture at the generic drawing of the British playwright above the door where they entered and paused to read the sign aloud. "Shakespeare and Company, Antiquarian Books."

Chapter 27.

THIS PARIS LANDMARK, Klewe explained to Zelda, was far more than the city's largest store for English-language books. Shakespeare and Company was a gathering place for locals and pilgrims, jammed with an unlikely array of customers vying to see its several overstocked rooms of books. The store was known for generously providing lodging to wayward and would-be writers struggling for the sake of their art. But what always left Klewe spellbound was the series of rooms loaded with such an eclectic choice of volumes. He stretched past Zelda to a reference shelf and removed a thick dictionary on English etymology.

"What do you know about the word 'ebony'?" he asked her, shuffling pages to that entry.

"Not much. Dark and beautiful like the wood."

"This dictionary says it may be connected to the word 'Hebrew.' Others say it means 'poison.'"

"So?" She leaned against a wide set of shelves. "Am I supposed to be shocked by that?"

"If I wanted to shock you, I'd have suggested you look up the origin of 'vanilla.' You know, that stuff you like in your vodka," he teased in return.

Zelda noticed a stoop-shouldered woman on the same aisle. "These Americans," she said to the elderly shopper, "they can be such prudes."

"Tell me about it," a wiry diminutive man in faded dungarees grunted as he eased his way past them. From the estimable stack of books the man was balancing, Klewe decided he must be a store clerk and stopped him to inquire about Mason Everly. The man listened to his request patiently. "No, I'm afraid there's been nobody here by that name," he said, trying to move along the crowded aisle. Although his English was impeccable, there was still enough accent to remind customers that this was quintessentially a French store.

"We don't think he came to Paris himself," Klewe tried to explain more precisely. "But he may have been planning to meet somebody here, possibly another Shakespeare teacher." While the older worker considered, a young Frenchman wearing a cowboy hat and brown pleather jacket intercepted Zelda at a tall shelf nearby.

Klewe heard the young man asking her, "May I be of assistance?" When he turned to observe, Zelda was on tiptoe trying to wrestle a book from a high shelf. "This one?" The Frenchman fingered a short volume while she indicated the enormous one next to it. "How stupid of me," he said, aiming his hand to his head and pulling a pretend trigger. The young man rubbed his scraggly growth of chin hair, a reddish-brown soul patch, before taking down the book she wanted and placing it on a lower shelf for her to examine.

"No," the clerk said emphatically to Klewe again and turned his attention back to the volumes he was carrying through the store.

"What did you find?" Klewe said to Zelda, as she smiled flirtatiously at the cowboy wannabe.

"This is called a concordance for Shakespeare," she said, sweeping a hand extravagantly across its thousand pages of fine text. "Every single word he wrote, and where each word appears in which play or poem." She held the volume up for him. "I never knew anybody had put together a book like this."

He nodded. "It's one of my all-time favorite resources. Amazing what it can tell you too. For all of the anti-black sentiment of his day, Shakespeare used the word 'black' some 200 times in his writings, far more than any other color. And dozens of times more than he used 'white,' its closest rival."

"Doesn't sound like Shakespeare had too much against it."

"No, it doesn't. In fact, it's in the very first line of what may have been his very first play, the start of his trilogy on Henry the Sixth. 'Hung be the heavens with black,' he wrote. How's that for describing the nighttime?" He was scouring the store for other employees, but the bearded youth was the only one who came near when Zelda smiled over at him again.

"Would you please reshelve this for me?" she said, pressing the concordance into his strong grip. "And where do you have books on Shakespeare himself?"

"I cannot tell you. I do not work here," he started to explain, but her question seemed to catch his interest. "What is it you are wanting to know?"

"Anything, really."

"I wish I could be of more help, Mademoiselle."

His eyes twinkled at her, but he said nothing more. Instead, he tipped his hat and walked rapidly away to an adjoining room where a piano was being played to entertain the store's varied customers.

"Must have been something you said," Klewe teased her.

"Apparently."

They took turns questioning other people inside the store. Klewe even took a few moments to scan notices on a bulletin board to see if some literary festival or activity might have been drawing his colleague's attention. Nothing seemed pertinent to the search, however, and he soon dismissed the idea of finding out anything in the bookshop.

"Let's go," he called to Zelda and opened the front door to leave. They were almost blinded outside by the intense sunlight of the Paris street and stood there motionless beside a green fountain, neither one sure what to do next.

"May I be of assistance?"

The two spun about to find the bearded young man again tilting his cowboy hat toward Zelda.

"I am Pierre Camion. At least," he added with an ingratiating smile, "that is my stage name. I am a student here in the city of Paris."

"A student," Klewe repeated skeptically. "Of what?"

Camion proffered another dazzling grin. "Acting, especially in the great cinema. You know, Peter Lorre and Humphrey Bogart. And the great John Wayne." He fired imaginary pistols into the air and tapped his hat. "Or Tom Cruise."

"Yes, I always think of Tom Cruise when I think of cowboys." Zelda returned the engaging smile.

"Perhaps I can be of service while you are in Paris," Camion told them, turning from Zelda to Klewe and back. "I'll show you our City of Lights and charge you only—how do you say?—a pittance."

Klewe was scanning the street beyond Camion to find another taxi. "You won't charge us anything. We're not going."

"Why not, Chris?" Zelda interceded on the young man's behalf.

"You just like all that attention he's giving you."

"What attention?" she said, failing to sound as innocent as she tried.

Klewe put his palm up to dismiss the persistent Frenchman. "Thanks anyway, and best of luck with your acting."

Camion thought for a long moment and then hitched his thumb back over his shoulder at the entrance to the bookstore.

"Are you certain, Monsieur?" he asked Klewe. "I could be of help to you. For example, are you sure you have the right Shakespeare and Company?"

Chapter 28.

"THE RIGHT ONE?" Klewe blurted out, taken aback by the young Frenchman's implication. "You mean this isn't the only Shakespeare and Company?"

Pierre Camion pushed the Stetson farther back on his forehead and dramatically uplifted his palms. "Not at all. This is merely the latest location for our most famous store of English books. Perhaps you have heard of Miss Sylvia Beach."

"Of course. It was originally her store, wasn't it? Started after World War One, I believe."

The French student nodded. "And did you know she was also the one to help publish the great James Joyce?" Camion swung his right arm forward to show the thick book he was carrying. It was a paperback copy of "Ulysses" that Sylvia Beach had bankrolled through its initial printing in 1922. "We might not have this book if not for her assistance." Camion avidly turned pages in the novel to find a specific passage. "Here is where he even mentions it as 'Shakespeare and company.'"

"How about that?" Zelda marveled, staring at the page. "An actual word from the sponsor. But can you help find the right building for us?"

"But of course."

"Then perhaps we do need a guide," Klewe conceded. He offered the drama student a handful of euros. "Will this pay for it?"

Camion pocketed the euros without counting them. "It would be my honor."

"Now what can you tell us about Sylvia Beach's bookstore?"

The Frenchman gave the store's green façade a sweep of his left arm and proclaimed in the formal tones of a tour guide, "This is not her store. At least, it is not the Shakespeare and Company she opened, but it does maintain the original name as an homage to Sylvia Beach."

"Okay," Klewe responded. "Then can you take us to the original location?"

"It was opened one place, then moved to another. Which would you like to see first?"

"Whichever came first, I guess."

"Very well then. We'll go this way," Camion said, toting the volume of Joyce while the two Americans tried to keep up with his rapid gait through the Latin Quarter. He charged along the street like a rampaging bull, his left hand free to gesticulate wildly at their surroundings. With each abrupt turn in direction, his deeply resonant voice would announce the new street with "Next!"

"Are you really a tour guide?" Zelda called to him breathlessly, in hopes of diminishing his stride through the crowded sidewalks of the Left Bank. They dodged tourists with strollers and a helmeted Segway rider who inadvertently scattered a clustering of sparrows and starlings with the personal transporter.

Over his shoulder, he answered back without slowing, "A little of this and a little of that. My parents, they do not approve of my endless education, so now I make money however I can, and I pay for my own books and tuition. That way I can study drama or whatever I like."

Camion turned left onto rue de la Huchette and hurried them past the open shops and onrushing customers before making another sharp left onto Saint-Michel. There the inviting scents of fresh-baked bread and pastries momentarily derailed their progress.

"His father sounds like Shakespeare's," Zelda commented to Klewe on the run as she offered him a bite of croissant. "Not a big theater fan."

Her remark caused Camion to stop instantly in his fast-moving tracks, and they came perilously close to colliding with him on the sidewalk. "I too have thought that," he told them. "My father has no use for drama, but my mother, well, she always loved the stage. I did not want to cause any conflict, so I have long tried to be—I don't know the English word for paying my own way."

"Self-sufficient?" Zelda volunteered, and he nodded.

"Perhaps someday I may even be recognized as the world's oldest student. Is there not a book of such feats?"

"The Guinness book of records," Zelda said, leaning against a signpost to adjust one of her half-boots and worry about a blister being formed by their speed walking. "But I don't know if that's a category. I imagine Shakespeare must be in there, isn't he?"

Klewe thought for a moment. "They've used his 'To be or not to be' soliloquy to test the world's fastest talkers. I think a Canadian set the record at something like 11 words a second."

Camion grinned. "I cannot quote it that fast, but I know the speech well. I have also learned some of his love poetry."

Formally removing his cowboy hat in the middle of the Paris sidewalk, he knelt down beside Zelda and started reciting to her with a heavy accent. "'Shall I compare thee to a summer's day?'" A cacophony of car horns provided occasional counterpoint to his delivery. Several pedestrians pushed by, giving him dirty looks for blocking their path, while others slowed to listen. Klewe stood there silently, perplexed all the way through the French student's impromptu performance, but he noticed how Zelda was thoroughly enjoying herself. When Camion finished with "'So long lives this, and this gives life to thee,'" a few of the onlookers broke into applause, and one passerby dropped a few coins into the cowboy hat in his outstretched hand.

Laughing together, the three turned onto a side street and then a second one even more dark and narrow, each announced by Camion with a dramatic "Next!" The tour became a blurred pastiche of footbridges, railed balconies and awnings. Finally they stopped short in front of the tinted windows for a shop on rue Dupuytren.

"Here we are," the drama student declared their arrival.

They stood staring into the entrance of a fashionable hair salon. For a moment nobody spoke.

Finally, Zelda broke the silence. "Next."

Camion seemed puzzled. "This too is not the one you seek?"

"No offense," Klewe said, "but I doubt my colleague would have interrupted his research for a haircut. Did you say there's another location?" He craned his neck to see the way back to a major thoroughfare.

"The other location, it is not far from here. But first," Camion said, leading their way into a blind alley nearby, "I have something I must say to you." He jammed his hand roughly into the pocket of his brown jacket and lowered his voice as he glared at the two Americans before him. "Give me the money."

Chapter 29.

THE STARE COMING from Pierre Camion's eyes remained as relaxed and friendly as before, but the words had turned to daggers. Nobody else could be seen walking along this deserted Paris alleyway. They had allowed themselves to be separated from the noontime crowds, and now no one would be close enough to help them.

Klewe stepped protectively closer to Zelda. He reached into his blazer pocket for the folded euros he still carried and slowly handed them to Camion.

The French student studied the money carefully, until his grimace turned into a grin and then raucous laughter.

"Oh, you Americans," he chuckled, handing the money back to Klewe. "You are too easy." He patted a stiff-shouldered Klewe on the arm. "Did you not recognize my Tom Cruise? 'Give me the money.' No, wait, that's not it." He thought for a second and corrected himself. "'Show me the money.' Yes, that's the line, is it not?"

Zelda and Klewe looked at each other in bewilderment and started to back away from Camion.

"I am sorry," he said, looking contrite about the ruse. With his free hand, he again pointed his finger at his own temple like a gun and fired the imaginary trigger with his thumb. "How stupid I am. It is all my fault. Here." He pulled the euros that Klewe had already paid him from his pocket and returned them to the startled couple. "I give you my tour free for frightening you so. Next," he said, beckoning to the left and ushering them back toward a well-traveled boulevard.

"Is this another trick?" Zelda asked Klewe.

Camion turned his palms upward. "Of course not. I give you my word. As a Frenchman."

The two Americans exchanged questioning looks but obligingly followed after him. Reluctantly, they allowed themselves to be guided back into the more populated streets of Paris to the frenetic flow of Camion's narration.

"You see," the student elaborated, "what most people do not know is that Shakespeare and Company moved twice to reach its present location. Between the one we have just visited and the current store, it was located for a very long time on rue de l'Odeon. It's not far at all, and I shall take you there." Making a turn at another corner, he shouted, "Next!"

Again he took off at a running walk, with the others almost jogging to keep pace with him. A swift mix of shops and traffic accentuated the speed of their movements. They had not gone far, but Zelda and Klewe were both breathing hard by the time they turned onto Saint-Germain. Ahead of them they spotted a corner café in the next block and requested a brief respite from the tour.

"Are you certain?" Camion asked. "The building you seek is only another street over from here."

"We'll get there soon enough," Klewe said, exhaling as he collapsed into a canvas-backed chair outside the café. "Who wants water?"

"Buzzkill," Zelda taunted. "How about vanilla vodka?"

Surrendering to their decision, Camion joined them at the table. "I am a mere student," he reminded them, sitting heavily in a chair opposite. "I am in no hurry." He dropped his copy of "Ulysses" onto the checkerboard tablecloth in front of him and propped the chair up against the building. "What shall we discuss?"

Zelda had already tumbled breathlessly into a third chair and removed a boot to rub her tired foot. "We were discussing the word 'ebony' in the Shakespeare bookstore."

The French student smiled, sparking to the subject. "Perhaps you have read Proust's dictionary. He writes of the biggest clichés in language, and one of them is 'as black as ebony.' Makes me think of the great black actors you have in America. Denzel Washington, for example." He frowned. "I do not know if he has done any Shakespeare."

"Yes, he has," Klewe said. "I saw him on Broadway a few years ago, playing a very dynamic Julius Caesar."

Camion gave a quizzical look. "Was Julius Caesar black? It makes no difference, of course, so long as the acting is good."

"That's true," Klewe nodded. "I once saw 'Othello' at the Shakespeare Theater in Washington. They had reversed all the racial casting, so they had a white Othello living in an all-black society. Shakespeare's story still works well despite switching the races around."

"That play does have a strong intrigue," Camion added. "No, not intrigue. How do you say that? A strong plot. It is universal."

"Shakespeare must have known how good the story was," Zelda agreed, waving repeatedly to get the staff's attention. Finally, a fidgety waiter enmeshed in an avocado apron came up to their table.

"Shall we have something to eat as well?" Camion asked. He rubbed the back of one hand against his soul patch. "My treat."

"It's on me, whatever you want," Klewe told them both, then turned to Zelda. "While Pierre is ordering, I think we should go take a look at the other location for Shakespeare and Company." He asked the French student, "You say it's around this corner?"

While Camion gave him directions, Zelda forced her foot back into the boot and lifted her bag, following along uncertainly.

"Why didn't you want Pierre to come with us?" Zelda asked when they were far enough from the café to assure privacy. "And next time remind me to wear my Skechers. These designer knockoffs are killing my feet."

"I'm not really sure we can trust him, especially after that business at the last address."

"That was bizarre, wasn't it?"

"He may be harmless enough, but remember that passage in 'Ulysses' he showed you? In that same chapter, Joyce refers to Shakespeare's three biggest villains—Iago in 'Othello,' King Richard the Third and the bastard Edmund in 'King Lear'—as Shakespeare's 'trinity of black Wills.'" Zelda's mouth dropped open. "So I do have to wonder if our friend is still playing us."

"But he's seemed to know what he's talking about where these stores are concerned."

"People always know more than they're willing to say. Meanwhile this whole thing smacks of a set-up. He's too old to be a student, he just happens to be reading 'Ulysses' when we run into him and he knows the exact address for a 90-year-old store? It's not just him, though. I'm not sure we should trust anyone here, so let's downplay the Shakespeare talk."

Zelda acquiesced. "You may be right about not trusting people," she said, pausing to survey the older neighborhood around them, with cars packed tightly along either side of the narrow street. "Still it's hard for me to believe there could be much racism in a place as cosmopolitan as this."

"Really? Tell me something. Are you an Oprah Winfrey fan?"

"I love her," Zelda gushed. "I'd bet you never even watched her show."

"You'd lose that bet. Years ago, Oprah told her audience that her summer reading list included Shakespeare, because it challenged her. You have no idea how much mileage teachers got out of that single recommendation."

"So what about her?"

"Remember how she was treated by a Paris shop a few years back? There was media outrage when a store refused to let her in after hours because they had been having trouble with what they called 'North Africans.'"

"I'd almost forgotten about that."

"I bet Oprah hasn't." He stopped at the address on rue de l'Odeon that Camion had given him. "Damn, it looks empty. I don't think we're going to find Mason's trail here. Might as well go back and relax."

Klewe started for the corner, but Zelda was not with him. He retraced his steps to where she stood in silence, seemingly entranced.

"What's wrong?"

"Your French is a lot better than mine," she insisted. "What does the sign on that building mean to you?"

Zelda pointed her index finger toward a small square sign down the street. It marked the entrance to a rundown building apparently under renovation. The façade was faded, wedged in between two bigger structures, and across the front door was affixed the name of the new occupant.

L'Ecole de Nuit.

Klewe's eyes enlarged rapidly as he translated the words.

"The School of Night."

Chapter 30.

KLEWE STARED AT the name transfixed, stalling for time. On the one hand, he knew he would have missed seeing the sign altogether without Zelda's assistance. On the other, he knew all too well what her next move would be, regardless of the danger.

Zelda, however, had no such dilemma. She was clearly prepared to make the most of her sudden find.

"I don't suppose," he said, "I could talk you into going back to the café and waiting for me there."

"Not a chance," she insisted. With a flourish, she pushed another stick of gum into her mouth and slipped the wedding ring that was inside her bag back onto her finger. "Shall we beat on?"

He exhaled heavily. "Boats against the current."

They edged themselves between the parked cars and walked across the narrow street to the dilapidated entranceway. The wooden door had rusted hinges, but it slowly pushed open far enough for them to get inside.

Heavy black drapes hung from the windows and walls inside the School of Night. As they stepped into a dimly lit anteroom, Zelda and Klewe instinctively moved close together to present a united front. They neared the reception desk with short nervous steps and waited for their presence to be acknowledged.

"Bonjour?" said a woman in her late 50's with cropped black hair and rounded hazel eyes. Presumably the school's secretary, she sat stiffly upright on a wheeled chair behind the desk and raised her head briefly from her paperwork to inspect the uninvited visitors. She was wearing a purple pastel business suit, and the eau de toilette that she exuded filled the sparse room with a heavy fragrance of lilacs. Before speaking with them again, she moved her new Louis Vuitton handbag off the desk and placed it, they both noticed, well out of their reach.

"Do you speak English?" Her response to Klewe was a curt nod, so he proceeded with a relieved smile. "Good. I'll spare you my attempts at French."

The expression that she presented him was deliberately cold. "Are you here about our school? I am Blanche Corneille," she introduced herself, "secretary for l'Ecole de Nuit. We are not as yet open for business."

"You have a lovely name," Klewe said. "Corneille, like the French playwright?"

"Yes, the greatest of all French dramatists."

"You might call him the French Shakespeare," Zelda suggested.

Blanche gave her a withering look. "We prefer to call Shakespeare the English Corneille." She diverted her greenish-brown eyes to Klewe. "How may I be of assistance to you?"

"Glad you asked," Zelda replied, making a deliberate show of her ring. "We are Christopher and Zelda. My husband," she said, indicating Klewe with a toss of her head, "and I were curious about your school's students."

"Our students are young men and women," the secretary explained, "of whom much is expected." She added ominously, "In our school, however, failure is not an option."

"Is that so?" Klewe listened, enjoying her accent. "Mostly, however, we need information about a friend who may have been here to visit your school."

"I see," she said, inviting them to sit on metal folding chairs facing her desk. "You must forgive the discomforts. We are moving in and, as you can see, still in the midst of refurbishing." She walked to a corner cabinet to pull a bottle and two glasses from inside. Handing each guest a small glass of red wine, she placed before them a tray of sliced cheese. "This is the best we can offer our visitors. And what is the name of this friend you are seeking?"

"Mason Everly."

Blanche pondered the name carefully, but she eventually shook her head. "No, I have met no one of that name. Why might he have come here to see us?"

Before Klewe could answer, Zelda interrupted apologetically. "Might you have some bread or crackers to go with this? My husband and I have been traveling all day, and we're famished."

He gave Zelda a wide-eyed stare as Blanche rose from the swivel chair again. "We may have something in the back. If you'll pardon me?" As she left the room, they could see a long empty hallway beyond her.

Left temporarily by themselves, Klewe spun around to face her. "What was that about? I don't want crackers. And I'm not your husband, Mrs. Klewe."

"I know that," Zelda said quickly. "I just wanted to get rid of her long enough to tell you something."

"What?"

She hopped up from the chair to look at the papers stacked on Blanche's desk. "Don't drink the wine."

"Thanks. I didn't plan to."

He took both of their wine glasses and set them aside on Blanche's desk. Zelda intensified her search, eventually unearthing several fax pages from a desktop pile.

"I don't trust that woman," she said, "no matter how sweet she smells." Her eyes quickly scanned the faxes, one of which she was still reading when Blanche came back into the room. Zelda dropped the page onto the edge of the desk to lift an antique picture frame. "What a pretty child! Is it your daughter?"

"She was. Lila passed away years ago." She reached across to take the frame from Zelda's hands and delicately realigned it on her desk.

"I'm sorry to hear that."

"We both are," Klewe added. "We were wondering, though, if we might speak to whoever is in charge of your school."

"Monsieur Corbeau is what you would call our school's headmaster, but he cannot possibly see you this afternoon. Perhaps you would care to make an appointment for tomorrow? He is quite busy, though."

"We wouldn't be taking up much of his time. And the matter, I assure you, is most urgent."

Blanche picked up the receiver of a large old-fashioned office telephone and punched a button that failed to illuminate. Then she made a soft-voiced request into the phone and awaited a reply. "No," she told Klewe decisively, hanging up. "I am afraid not. It might be hours before the headmaster could see you today."

"That's all right," Zelda answered, not seeming the least discouraged. "I'll have time to read today's International Herald-Tribune." She looked around her chair and gave out a disheartened sigh. "That is, if my husband here will bring me a copy of the paper." She smiled sweetly at Klewe. "Honey, could you get me an I.H.T. to read while I wait?"

A digital 24-hour clock in the largely unfurnished office indicated it was almost an hour past noon. Zelda stood up beside Blanche's desk and draped her hand onto the piece of paper she had been holding before.

"I hope it's all right," she said to Blanche, "if I wait here?"

Doubtfully, Blanche began, "I do not think there is much reason, Madame, but if you wish." She instantaneously returned to sorting the documents atop her desk.

Klewe could not tell what Zelda was planning, but he watched carefully as she slid her hand off the edge of Blanche's desk. As she did, the fax page dropped noiselessly onto the floor, and Zelda began chewing her gum more vigorously. Once she caught his attention, she directed his eyes to the fallen page. He tried spearing it using the end of his umbrella, but without success.

He stood up to leave. Both he and Blanche were startled when Zelda called out loudly for him to wait, her voice filled with surprising urgency. She crossed the office under Blanche's steady gaze and unnerved Klewe when she seized him by the shoulders. He was even less prepared when she held him to her and planted a long passionate kiss on his mouth.

Chapter 31.

FOR AN EXTENDED moment, the kiss between them lingered, Zelda pressing her lips passionately to Klewe's. And then, just as impulsively, she drew back from him.

"Newlyweds," she explained to a querulous Blanche. "It's hard to be apart, even for a half hour." Klewe caught the time reference. At the same instant he also realized that during the kiss she had transferred the chewing gum from her mouth into his.

Zelda delicately rolled her eyes toward the floor, but at first he did not comprehend her signal. When Blanche stopped looking at them, she mimed the act of chewing until he understood.

As surreptitiously as he could, Klewe removed the gum from his mouth and let it fall onto the paper. Then he stepped squarely with his right foot on the gum, its sticky substance sealing the page to the sole of his shoe. Once he was outside the school door, he angled himself against the building to remove the paper, regretfully thinking how much he'd paid for the Hush Puppies he was wearing. He extricated the page as cleanly as he could and wiped the sole of his loafer against the curb.

With great reluctance he left Zelda inside the school and returned to the sidewalk café to wait with Pierre Camion. There the

Paris student sat, aimlessly leaning his chair against the front wall of the building, his cowboy hat pushed high on his brow.

"Ah, my friend, you have come back," Camion said with a wide grin, inviting Klewe to sit. "I have been listening to a tune by Jimmy Buffett and decided to order us a bottle of tequila. Care for a drink?"

"'Five o'clock somewhere,'" Klewe quoted, rubbing his hands together in anticipation. He explained to Camion that Zelda was awaiting an appointment. Then he spread out the gum-smudged paper, which he found no less readable for the subterfuge. It was, he discovered, written in French and faxed from Mason Everly to M. Corbeau in Paris, but without indication of the school's name.

"I no longer plan to visit Paris this week," Klewe translated Everly's words silently, "so I must decline the kind invitation to come by your.school. I do intend, however, to meet at noon Saturday with your friend Earl at the Globe in London. I will deliver my talk there that evening and wish you could attend." Everly had signed the note, which was date-stamped two days before his death.

By now, a bottle of Jose Cuervo, along with three shot glasses, had been delivered by the waiter, who paused to see whether food was also to be ordered. Camion declined the food and set up two glasses of the Tequila Oro. "Tell me more about Shakespeare's family, which does sound a bit like mine. I would think his father was most unhappy with his decision to work in the theater."

"Probably. The family business of making and selling gloves in Stratford was more likely what his father had in mind for him, but he ended up working in the London playhouses. I doubt his father was overjoyed at that prospect." He opened his pocket watch and looked anxiously up the street. "I hope Zelda is doing all right."

"Why wouldn't she be? We could go now, though, if you like."

"In half an hour, she said, and it hasn't been that long yet. I'm wondering, though, about leaving her there." As he finished speaking, he saw a familiar figure rushing along the sidewalk on the other side of the street. The flashing eyes were focused on the ground, but it was clearly Blanche Corneille, her arm freely swinging the new Louis Vuitton handbag as she darted along. When she briefly looked up, the frozen smile on her face dissolved as soon as she spotted Klewe. Just as quickly, though, her surprised expression was replaced by the implacable smile, and she clutched the white purse possessively as she went on her way.

Camion let out a whistle as she passed. "Who was that?" he asked.

"She's the secretary," Klewe said, self-conscious of how unnatural his English words must sound to a native Frenchman. "For a new school near that last address you gave us. That's where Zelda is now, waiting to talk with the headmaster."

"Very attractive, I must say," Camion smiled, not taking his eyes off the secretary. "What is her name, in case I decide to enroll?"

"I don't know about enrolling, but her name is Blanche Corneille."

"I see," he said with delight. "Corneille? You mean like our great French playwright? I borrowed the name Pierre from him."

"How's that?"

"For my stage name, of course. It's Pierre Camion." The French student poured the Oro again. "I have always loved his work. And the name Corneille sounds so evocative, does it not?" He turned the bottle around to show Klewe. "See the name on this brand? Corneille translates into Spanish as 'Cuervo.' Over the years I have won many drinking bets by knowing Jose Cuervo is the Spanish for what you Americans would call 'Joe Crow.' How do you like that?"

Klewe nearly choked on a swallow from the shot glass. "What are you saying?"

"Pierre Corneille's name would be—how would you say it in English?—yes, that's it. Peter Crow."

"My God," Klewe gasped as the pieces flew into place in his mind. "And Blanche is the French for white?"

"Yes, that's what Blanche means. Much like that color you seem to be turning, my friend."

Klewe, however, missed the mention of his chameleon complexion, because he was already on his feet and running.

Chapter 32.

"ZELDA!" KLEWE'S THROAT sounded hoarse from shouting, having called her name repeatedly as he ran back to the dilapidated school building. He shoved against its heavy front door, which yielded begrudgingly to his shoulder. "Zelda, are you all right?"

There inside the anteroom sat Zelda Hart on the same folding chair, her stunned expression reflecting into his relieved eyes. "Why wouldn't I be?"

He collapsed into the chair next to her with a drastic intake of oxygen. She looked expectantly at him, awaiting some breathless declaration of concern for her. At last, he caught his breath.

"Thanks for the gum," he said.

"Oh, that. I'm not usually that forward. Okay, maybe I am, but I figured that desperate times called for—"

Klewe cut her off in mid-sentence and rose to leave. "Let's get out of here," he told her, "before Blanche Corneille comes back." In halting words, he translated the secretary's name as "White Crow," expecting Zelda to react with trepidation.

"And?" she asked flatly.

"You don't find that disturbing?"

"Because she lied about who she is? I did too."

He could not fault her logic there, so he tried another angle. "When is she supposed to be coming back?"

"I don't know. She called someone on the phone before she left. I'm not sure what they were talking about, but it sure sounded like she wanted to pay somebody for a cat, whatever that means. Why can't the French speak in plain English?"

"Well, I don't know about that. But I'm not at all sure she believes you're my wife."

"Calm down. Even if she is White Crow, she's gone for now. I'm still waiting for this Corbeau person to see me." She sat back and crossed her legs. "And I don't intend to leave without some answers. For that matter, what did the fax have to say? I saw your friend's name on it, but I don't read French."

"Mason wrote that he'd decided against coming here to speak with Corbeau. He was planning to meet someone named Earl at the Globe Theater tomorrow. For some reason, though, he decided to come back to the States first."

"Then maybe we shouldn't be looking for answers here in Paris. Is that all it said?"

"Yes. And I'm heading to London next. By myself."

"Not yet," she gestured for him to take a seat, ignoring his last comment. "Corbeau may be the key to all this. I want to know what he knows. Or you could ask Blanche. She did seem somewhat taken with you."

"That's ridiculous."

"Is it? Oh, well, maybe we shouldn't wait for Corbeau to come to us. Shall we just help ourselves?" she asked, standing up. "Blanche said he was busy, but maybe—" As she was crossing the floor, Zelda's shoe became entangled in the phone cord from Blanche's desk. Instead of causing her to trip, however, the cord gave way under her foot. It reminded Klewe that the secretary's phone failed to light up during the earlier call.

"Wait a second," he said pensively to Zelda and knelt down behind Blanche's desk. "She wasn't calling anybody from this phone. It's not even connected." From beneath the desk, he observed crumpled pieces of brown wrapping paper. The wrapping was stamped PE-4.

"So how could she call Corbeau in his office?" Zelda wondered.

Klewe lifted himself to his feet and, in a voice beginning to show panic, ordered her to back out of the building. "Was Blanche saying 'pay a cat,' by any chance?"

"Why? What's the matter with you?"

"I think I know what 'pay a cat' is French for." He pushed her toward the street entrance while he stealthily opened the hallway door opposite. "And I don't believe we'll find Corbeau back there. Have you noticed how quiet it is?"

He called out the man's name, but the building remained silent. Down a darkened hallway he could barely see the outline of a closed office door with "M. Corbeau" printed on the front. He strained for a moment until his eyes adjusted to the dimness. Midway along the corridor, he finally spotted a short piece of wire stretched across the floor a few inches high. Anxiously he gestured for Zelda to open the front door.

"Just wait for me outside. Please." He looked about the office and noticed the wheels on the secretary's chair. Cautiously, he rolled it around the desk and into the hallway.

"What's that for?" Zelda asked, cracking open the door to the street. He made no response. "Chris? What are you going to do?"

"Blow the whole place up," he answered at last, twisting the chair about and hurling it on its wheels down the hall. As soon as his hands let the chair fly, he shoved Zelda backward out of the building, diving onto the front sidewalk as they braced for the explosion.

Chapter 33.

"MERDE!" EXCLAIMED A loud voice close at hand. It was an outraged Parisian whose bag of fresh groceries now lay scattered across the walk. Klewe turned to check on Zelda, who stopped him from translating the befuddled man's tirade, a veritable stream of foreign expletives followed by a word she recognized as "Americans."

"Never mind," she told Klewe. "I understand more French than I thought."

They muttered apologetically with what little French they could muster to the startled shopper, both of them bending down to recover his fallen produce. Tomatoes and cucumbers had rolled several feet from the door, and a few eggs lay broken and dripping in their carton. Klewe offered several euros to reimburse the man, who moved along clutching whatever was left in his grocery bag.

"Thank God," Klewe told Zelda. "I thought for sure we were both dead."

"What gave you that idea?"

He recounted the trip wire he had seen, along with the PE-4 packaging under the secretary's desk. "The French P is pronounced 'pay,'" he explained, "and the number four is 'quatre,' which made Blanche's PE-4 sound like 'pay a cat.'"

"But what is it?"

"Plastic explosives. Similar to our C-4, but used more in Britain."

While he was still explaining, Zelda noticed a fast-approaching gendarme and took Klewe by the elbow to walk him briskly away from the prying eyes of the French police.

"Which way is Pierre?" she asked, and he indicated the way back to the café on the next street. When they arrived back there, Camion still sat against the front wall, but the tequila had clearly taken effect. His chair was tipped back, the cowboy hat pitched low across his face for a nap.

Softly they reseated themselves at the table. Across the sidewalk from them at another table sat an elderly French couple engrossed in their afternoon meal. The old man, his hands struggling unevenly, was leaning over the table to help cut a slice of beef into manageable bites for his wife.

"See that?" Zelda whispered to Klewe. "That's what I want."

"Roast beef?"

"No, silly. Somebody to count on. That's what marriage vows really mean, once you get past the flowery words and sentiment. I don't think that's too much to hope for. Wouldn't Shakespeare have agreed?"

"I guess so." Klewe spoke quietly, trying not to disturb Camion's rest. "Of course, he may not have been the most loyal of husbands."

"Not if he abandoned his wife with three small children to bring up by herself."

"He did go to London, but that doesn't mean he never went home to care for his family. He certainly made enough money to support them. But you're right, he may well have had a wandering heart. We do know, for instance, that he addressed several of his sonnets to a woman who fascinated him, and it probably wasn't his wife."

"Who was she?"

"We know her as the Dark Lady."

Zelda's eyes grew wide again. "And nobody's found that odd about him?"

"Not really. The Dark Lady has been identified as various females in Elizabethan England, including a dark-skinned woman named Lucy Negro, who ran a London brothel."

"Well," she said, pouring the remaining tequila into their shot glasses, "I think it's time we toast your theory. To a whole new Shakespeare."

"We should include our friend here, don't you think?"

Klewe reached over to tap Camion's arm where it rested on the table. The student did not rouse. Instead, his arm fell off the table, dangling limply beside him.

Alarmed, Klewe lifted up the cowboy hat that covered Camion's face. It was only then that he could clearly see the Frenchman was not napping. They could also see where the blood had already begun to clot beneath what remained of his left ear.

THE FOURTH ACT:
SCHOOL OF NIGHT

Chapter 34.

AN EXHAUSTED ZELDA came suddenly awake and sat upright on a hardwood bench. Beside her slouched a sleep-deprived Klewe, waiting to complete his night-long argument with her.

"Go home," he repeated frequently to an intractable Zelda. "I'm asking you please to go home now."

They were sprawled on a bench inside Gare du Nord, a railway station in the northern part of Paris, their feet worn from walking the streets of the city into the middle of the night. Zelda waited for him to lower his voice before she responded.

"Are you serious? You talk about the importance of sacrificing everything for the truth, but you expect me to run at the first hint of danger."

"Hint?"

She ignored his sarcasm. "You're the one who's meant to uncover the real Shakespeare. I firmly believe that, just as I know I'm the one who's meant to cover the story. And that's that." She sat petulantly back against the bench and folded her arms. "Where's my bag?"

"Right here," he said, leaning forward to remove the Coach bag from behind him. "This train station can be a dangerous place during the nighttime, especially if you don't want the authorities finding you." He tried a kinder tone with her. "Look, Zelda, last evening we had to make an anonymous call to the Paris police to report Pierre's murder, and you're calling that a hint of danger. What do you consider actual danger?"

"We're safe enough here," Zelda surmised as she sized up the other dawn riders of the French railway.

"Safe? Not here or anywhere else. If the killer doesn't get us, the police probably will. At least three or four other people saw us throw some money on Pierre's table before we got up and ran." He saw her disappointment and lightened his tone again. "Maybe we'll be all right here till we get on the train. Nobody would have followed us from the café overnight. At least I hope not."

Zelda searched for her notebook and pen. "You're exhausted and so am I, but I still need to get all this down on paper. What were you telling me about Beethoven when we were out walking last night?"

"There was speculation a generation ago that the German composer was black. It's similar to Shakespeare's case, because everybody knows how Beethoven looked. Or they think they do from seeing a bust of him in the comic strip 'Peanuts.'"

They were sitting near a station newsstand, with posters advertising candies and cold drinks among its racks of newspapers and magazines. When Zelda completed her notes, she walked over to pick up a paperback book she spotted and flipped quickly through the pages. She placed it back, much to the chagrin of the newsstand owner, and retraced her steps to Klewe.

"I was afraid of that," she said, making another note.

"What?"

"That was a French-English dictionary. I looked up 'corbeau,' and it's a synonym for 'corneille.' Another French word for a crow."

Without commenting, Klewe stood up to stretch and count the growing number of passengers waiting for early-morning trains to arrive. Finally, he said, "The crowd isn't as rowdy here, but they remind me of the one in 'Sir Thomas More.' It's an Elizabethan drama, but not very famous. Ever heard of it?"

"I've heard of him, not the play."

"It includes a scene where the crowd is about to riot, because they're angry about the growing number of foreigners or 'strangers' in London. Sir Thomas More comes in to give a speech and is able to quell the rioting against the immigrants."

"And Shakespeare wrote it?"

"Well, no. Not the entire play. That's the interesting part. He apparently was called in only to rewrite this one mob scene. We know that, because we have it in his handwriting. In fact, it's the only scene of any play we have in Shakespeare's own hand. And the scene he rewrites is specifically about the importance of tolerating outsiders. It's as if he were an outsider on the inside, teaching his audience that difference shouldn't be attacked."

Zelda put away the pen and notebook. "I can't believe you're giving me such an amazing story to report."

"Let's hope it ends well," he said warily and dropped down into his seat. "I only wish I were more certain about all this."

"How's that?"

"I keep having doubts." He turned to Zelda. "People are dying, and I'm still skeptical. How can I put you in danger if I can't say I believe it?"

"That's the part I don't get," Zelda said frankly. "If you're so worried about me and all this danger, why not just announce your theory? You could go on the Internet right now and tell the whole world. There's nobody stopping you, and it would be instant safety, wouldn't it?"

Klewe considered her words carefully. "I could do that. I know it may sound foolish to you, but I owe this to Mason. When we first decided to make our big announcement at the Globe, you should have seen his eyes light up. You don't often spark a look like that in a mentor, somebody you've worked with and admired for years and years." He thought for a moment. "I need to do this for him."

"Then we will." She reassured him with a weary smile.

A moment later, a blaring message over the public-address system brought them both to their feet. "The first Eurostar to London," Klewe said. "That's our train."

Chapter 35.

ONCE ABOARD THE high-speed train to London, Klewe and Zelda managed to locate vacant seats next to each other. In the row opposite sat a young Japanese woman with long black hair and an elderly British woman for whom she was apparently the caregiver. The old woman's wrinkled face was buried in a mystery novel, and the two Americans decided nobody was paying attention to them.

"Should we have called Detective Robinson again?" Zelda nudged him as the train began to move slowly along the tracks.

Klewe shook his head. "Not yet. Try to relax for a couple hours." He looked around at the growing light outside the train windows. "Enjoy the scenery."

The caregiver across from Zelda took a ballpoint pen from her Meisei book bag and began writing numbers onto a puzzle clipped from a newspaper. Zelda bent forward to satisfy her curiosity.

"Kakuro?" Zelda asked.

The Japanese woman shook her head and responded, "Sudoku."

"Oh," Zelda said, sitting back. She indicated the empty ring finger of Klewe's left hand and repeated, "Sudoku," at which point both women laughed.

"Do you two provide subtitles?" he whispered. "You hadn't told me that you speak Japanese."

"That's because you've just heard my entire vocabulary. Those are the names of two puzzles that use numbers. They're the hottest thing these days. Kakuro isn't for me, though. Too much addition."

"Then what was so funny?"

"Oh, I'd read that Sudoku means 'single numbers.' I was telling her how unmarried you are."

"Thanks a lot."

For several moments, Zelda made no conversation, riding along seemingly lost in the passing landscape. At last, she asked him, "Could there be other descriptions or pictures of Shakespeare that may yet be found?"

"I hope so. I really hope there are, but I doubt it. And if anything is found, the problem will always be authenticating it. Four centuries have already passed by. That means 400 years of fakes and forgeries being marketed to make a quick fortune off the Bard. Have you heard of death masks, for instance?"

"Uh-huh. Those are plaster casts made from dead people's faces, aren't they? To preserve a likeness of somebody who died back in the days before photography."

"When the casts are legitimate, yes. But people have been willing to make false death masks of anybody and sell them as authentic likenesses of historical figures. The trouble is we have no idea whose masks they really are and no way to verify them."

They were already traveling through the outskirts of Paris. Morning sunlight began to flood the countryside while the pace of the train steadily increased.

"Don't forget," he added, "Shakespeare has always been big business. In the years after he died, there were dozens of works by other writers that were attributed to him to make a quick buck. Several plays and poems were printed under his name that we don't believe he wrote, some of them included in the later editions of the Folio. Scholars are still arguing over who wrote what. And, in addition to those, there were all kinds of fake letters and mementos for sale, ranging from supposed locks of the Bard's hair to rings that he may or may not have ever possessed."

"I know people can be like that today. But I never dreamed Elizabethan England would have had so many crooks and con men around."

"Believe it. History is replete with them. I remember reading once about the burial of John Milton. Another of England's greatest writers, but he apparently wasn't lucky about having his remains left undisturbed. After Milton died in the 17th century, grave robbers broke into the tomb to take away whatever they could. His skeleton was still intact at that point, so what do you think they did?"

When Zelda did not reply, the elderly British woman sitting across from Klewe put down her mystery and said, "They took his hair and broke out his teeth, they did, taking anything they thought they could sell." After a brief pause, she added, "Sorry to listen in on your conversation, but I'm a bit of a history fancier myself."

"That's all right," he assured her. "From what I've read, in the years after his death, you could find plenty of Milton's teeth for sale on the open market. About a hundred or so."

The old woman chuckled. "More than three times the number in any human mouth. You never can tell about some people." She returned to her reading.

"So that's why I don't hold out too much hope of finding an accurate Shakespeare portrait," he confided to Zelda. "I just wish I'd thought twice about getting other people involved in all this. That includes you."

"You can't possibly hold yourself responsible for what Mason chose to do," she said sensibly. "Besides, from what you've told me about him, he sounds a lot like you. He couldn't have been stopped either."

"And I've never even told you about some of the other research I've done. There's so much more to Shakespeare than any one person would ever be able to discover." He studied Zelda's patient expression. "I'm talking too much again, right?"

"Not at all. I love your passion when you talk about Shakespeare. Do you show that passion in your teaching?"

"You'd have to ask my students. Frankly, I don't know what they'd think if they saw me now, running around Europe with a beautiful woman."

Zelda's eyes glowed warmly. "I doubt they'd be all that surprised."

"Hell, I am. And I can't believe your marriage didn't take. Did eye trouble run in his family?"

"I like to tell myself that." She grew thoughtful. "I just don't understand what's wrong with people anymore," she said, her voice growing agitated. "I thought it was bad enough in America, and now we seem to be finding racism and prejudice everywhere we go."

"My dear child," the British woman interposed, closing her novel again to speak, "prejudice has no national boundaries. It's the most insidious power around. I live near London, and I can assure you that racism and other hateful acts are not just an American commodity. We have more than our share of shameful times in British history as well." She fluffed her bluish hair as she placed the book in her lap and bent past her Japanese caregiver. "Why, I could tell you stories that would make you sink nails into your young man's arm in fear. Some of my ancestors were Jewish, and the mistreatment of Jews in England over the centuries has been as bad as anything you can imagine. The tortures, the executions, the horrors they endured, it's all there in the history books."

Zelda nodded but said nothing. Tapping the armrest of her train seat, the old woman grew more insistent that she pay close attention to her words.

"In the year 1290, for instance, Edward the First issued an Edict of Expulsion, ordering all self-avowed Jews to leave England forever. The ethnic cleansing had already started, with large numbers of Jews hanged after being accused of coin clipping."

"What's that?" Zelda asked her.

"Trimming down the edges of gold and silver coins to keep more of the precious metals. But those deaths weren't enough. After Edward's proclamation, they gathered together as many Jews as they could find and prepared to make them leave England. Now, if you know anything about the Thames River in London, you may remember that it has high and low tides. At low tide, they made these poor unfortunate creatures, some of them my forebears, walk out into the Thames. Then the tide came back in, leaving the entire group to drown. No, do not talk to me of cruelty as a singularly American trait."

"That's terrible." Zelda shivered. "Have other Jews in British history been treated that harshly?"

"Some even worse. Elizabeth the First, for instance, had her own personal physician named Roderigo Lopez. He was a Jew from Portugal. A double whammy, you might say, for an outsider in those days. Some say Shakespeare used him as the model for Shylock. Anyway, the doctor wasn't treated badly, at least not while he was useful to the Tudor court. But then he became expendable too."

"What happened to him?"

"When Elizabeth became sick unexpectedly, they needed somebody to take the blame, so they decided her personal physician must be trying to poison her to help the Spanish overthrow her. He was arrested, tried and summarily executed, all on flimsy evidence."

"How awful."

"Let me tell you how awful it was. When they quartered him and removed his heart, they say he was still alive." Without awaiting a response, the older woman opened her mystery again.

Klewe bent across the seat to Zelda. "Now do you want out of this mess?"

She thought about it for a moment and shook her head. Then Zelda leaned over to kiss him gently. "Don't worry," she promised, "no gum this time."

They sat back and slept fitfully during the remainder of their trip, including their ride through the Chunnel. As the train began pulling into the London station later, they awoke to an abrupt stop on the tracks near St. Pancras International. From the front of their car, two officials in security outfits came onboard and wended their way through the aisle until halting specifically beside Zelda's seat.

After flashing identification, the men asked the two Americans for their names and passports, which they supplied. "You'll have to come with us," one of the men said. "Matter of routine inquiry."

Klewe reached under the seat for his umbrella as Zelda collected her shoulder bag, and they headed up the aisle escorted by the officials. Before disembarking, though, Zelda cast a final look back at their seat companions.

"They'd seemed nice enough," she heard the elderly British woman say without looking up from her novel.

The Japanese companion steadily returned Zelda's gaze until the moment the train doors started to close. Then she went back to working her Sudoku, pausing only long enough to say in perfect English, "You never can tell about some people."

Chapter 36.

"SPECIAL AGENT CHAMBERS?"

From a sitting position inside the train station, Klewe was shocked to recognize the imposing figure of an African American woman in a Burberry trenchcoat, and he stood bolt upright, his shoulders squared facing her.

Zelda's mouth opened slightly. "You two know each other?"

Klewe whispered back, "We met last year. In Williamsburg."

After railway security officers escorted them from the train at St. Pancras International, Eurostar's main terminal in London, they had been funneled into a claustrophobic backroom of the Victorian rail station. There they had been left waiting for more than an hour on hardbacked chairs in a windowless area. When the door finally did spring open, the woman in the trenchcoat confidently entered the small room and prepared to introduce herself.

Special Agent Wallie Chambers of the F.B.I. appeared to be in her mid-30's with dark skin and bright brown eyes, her silver-tinged hair styled short to frame her face. They waited silently for the woman, who had not yet smiled in their presence, to unbutton the gray coat she wore over a dark pantsuit. Finally, she spoke directly to Klewe, stepping forward to shake his hand. "Well, if it isn't the Shakespeare Sherlock."

"Don't start that," he said to her, then pointed to his companion. "This is Zelda Hart, a reporter."

"So," Wallie inquired of him with a quizzical smile, "how's Beverly?"

"Beverly, huh?" Zelda asked suspiciously.

"An administrator from William and Mary," he told Zelda, then turned back to Wallie. "Bev's fine, as far as I know."

"Sorry to hear that," she said with a gleam in her eye before asking Zelda, "How much has he told you about himself? That he stopped a serial killer? That the Klewes are among the oldest families in Virginia? Or that he's won every teaching award there is?"

"If you're completely through ratting me out," he addressed Wallie, "I do hope you've recovered from our last encounter."

"Why?" Zelda asked. "What happened?"

"I dislocated my shoulder," Wallie explained, catching Klewe's eye, "but it's healed nicely. Now I'd like to hear what's been happening with you."

While Wallie engaged Klewe in small talk about Virginia, Zelda retrieved a notebook and pen from her bag on a nearby table. Settling back onto the uncomfortable chair, she rolled up her turtleneck sleeves and began working what looked like math problems. Every few moments she would scratch through an answer with frustration and begin figuring again. After Wallie was called outside, Zelda slapped the notebook against her hand.

"What is it?" Klewe asked.

"Anagrams," she complained. "They can be maddening. But really addictive too. I was just working on 'Harry Potter' to see if there's any hidden message in that."

"Find any?"

She scrunched her face thoughtfully. "Well, of course, there is the obvious 'parry hotter,' but that's not exactly earthshaking."

"Not exactly."

"Then there's 'the Orr party.' Or 'her arty trope.'"

He thought for a second. "You have an extra letter in that last one, but it's good to know you've been working on something really important."

Zelda cast him a disdainful look and went on. "Here's my favorite, though. You remember how J. K. Rowling's books set sales records?"

"I remember Amazon-dot-com released its 10-year list of best-sellers awhile back, and Shakespeare came in 26th, just behind Tom Clancy. Not too shabby for someone who died in 1616."

"Still he's no Harry Potter," she said forthrightly. "How about 'trophy rater' for an anagram?"

He gave her a sidelong glance but made no comment.

"Hey, we don't even know what your friend here wants with us. Why are you determined to be unpleasant?"

"Maybe it's because I'm making the most important speech of my life tonight, almost completely unprepared, and we've been running from the police while I get ready."

"See? That doesn't sound so bad." She proffered an impish grin. "I'm just glad I won't be winging it in front of that big crowd this evening."

"I'm so happy for you."

"Oh, just tell them what you've told me. Start with the White Crow business and go from there."

"What are you two going on about?" Wallie Chambers was coming back into the room and balancing two cups of coffee, which she placed next to their seats.

"Look, Special Agent Chambers, how long—" he began, and the agent signaled him back into the hard chair next to Zelda.

"You can both call me Wallie. I'm in London to consult on security problems and help Scotland Yard with counter-terrorism measures. Thought maybe I could help you out too."

Zelda asked, "Then why have you arrested us?"

"Have you been arrested? So far you've only been served coffee. Think of this as a friendly detaining."

"How long are you planning to be so friendly?" Zelda took a sip and made a sour face at the brew.

"Not long." Then her brown eyes turned into slits, her voice growing suspicious. "Now what exactly were you discussing when I came in?"

Klewe warily tried changing the subject. "I was telling her about the Upstart Crow. It's a great bookstore in southern California."

"Didn't I hear you say something about White Crow?"

"Only that they want to kill us," Zelda interjected candidly. When Klewe tried to hush her, she turned angrily on him. "What good does it do us to stay quiet? That's what they're probably counting on." He rolled his eyes, but he stopped interrupting her. "We think they've killed three people already, and we're both on their list."

"We've had some intelligence reports about a terrorist cell called White Crow," Wallie told them.

Klewe exhaled loudly. "I thought so. Blanche Corneille's name couldn't be a coincidence."

"You're right. We've been monitoring Internet chatter about them and their umbrella organization." Wallie checked through her notes. "A school of some kind."

"The School of Night," Zelda informed her. She recounted their story from Washington to London, managing to cover the entire ordeal in unusually short order, while Klewe added a few salient details. By the time they had finished telling of Camion's murder in Paris, Wallie Chambers was staring at them in astonishment.

"And you think all of this has been done to keep you quiet about some Shakespeare theory?"

"I think a lot more than this has been done," Klewe replied. "I think we know only a small fraction of what's been going on."

"You think it all began with Sir Walter Raleigh?" Wallie asked, almost scornfully. "But that must be wrong."

"How can you be so sure? Zelda and I have been on the run because of Raleigh's School of Night or its White Crow cell or whoever these people are. I wouldn't arbitrarily rule out anyone, living or dead, who might be involved."

"Oh, that part I believe," she said, the sarcasm creeping into her tone. "I also think it's a larger group than you realize. What I don't know is how you believe you can outrun them. You must know how these conspiracy theories work. All those little space creatures and everything."

Klewe and Zelda looked at each other in exasperation. Finally, he said, "Yes, Wallie, the world is full of conspiracy theories, but we're running from people who have killed three of our friends, and we don't know how much longer we can keep going. In fact, I hope to stay alive at least until I give that talk at the Globe tonight."

"I'll make sure you're around for that," she promised him.

"Speaking of which, when exactly will we be allowed to go on our way?"

"Not just yet. I'll need to make a few calls to confirm your story." She walked pensively out of the room while Klewe and Zelda considered their next move.

After a few moments, Wallie returned, carrying a cell phone that she handed to Klewe. "It's for you."

He shot her a questioning glance.

"Somebody who's been dying to talk with you," she said and smiled meanly.

Chapter 37.

"PROFESSOR KLEWE? AT long last. It seems you for-
got to leave me your number in France. Or tell me you were going
there." The emphatic voice on the line was unforgettable, even
without its heavy tinge of disapproval.

"Hello, Detective."

Wallie had pressed the speaker button, allowing everyone in
the room to hear Edmund Robinson all the way from D.C., where
daylight had not yet begun to break. Zelda stared straight ahead
expressionless, while the Special Agent seemed to be awaiting some
long-distance fireworks.

The caller did not disappoint her. "Any news, Professor?
Perhaps something I should know about?"

Klewe looked around the cramped storage area in the London
train terminal. "No news here, Detective. Just sitting around chatting with your friend, Special Agent Chambers. May I ask why
you're calling?"

"It's not for phone sex," the detective bellowed trans-Atlantic,
almost without need of the phone. "Correct me if I'm wrong, but
didn't I tell you to report to my office two days ago?"

"Haven't had the chance, sir. Zelda's here too, and she hasn't
had a chance yet either."

"Hello, Detective," she chimed in beside him.

"By the way," Klewe said, "I did ask Zelda about those little matters you wanted me to clear up, and there was nothing to them."

"I am so relieved to hear that, Professor," Robinson replied, his voice growing heavier with sarcasm. "Now tell me what the hell is going on."

Zelda inhaled a big breath to launch into another telling of their story since leaving Washington. She ended with the death of Camion and their subsequent detention by Wallie in London, adding, "We suspect you have a hand in that last part."

"I sure do. So the School of Night that you found in Paris didn't offer you any new leads?"

"Not much," Klewe said. "Beyond Mason's fax to them, we have no evidence of a link to his death. But now we'll concentrate our search in London, which was the last place he was before Washington." He waited judiciously. "I don't suppose you'd have any new information you may want to share with us."

"I probably shouldn't. I should be ordering you back here, but since you were going to London anyway to make your friend's talk, I can tell you this. The murder weapon has been identified." The scratching sound of papers being rearranged came clearly across the telephone line. "A main-gauche. That's my lousy French for a 400-year-old dagger."

"As old as the School of Night," Klewe reminded him.

"That's why I'm telling you this. The more you look into it, the more dangerous it becomes. You might want to think about that."

"He has," Zelda said. "And he's tried to send me home at least twice. For the record, though, I plan on staying."

"See what I'm up against?" Klewe announced into the phone.

"I see. One more thing."

"What's that?"

"I tried to check that security guard in Foggy Bottom you questioned. Just to see what he might have to say sober."

"And?"

"And there is no Hal Iger."

"What?" he and Zelda asked together.

"There is no Hal Iger. Not with any agency or security firm inside or outside the Beltway. The man doesn't exist, and neither does Foggy Bottom Investigations."

Klewe looked over at Zelda, who was again grabbing paper and pen to work furiously at some writing. "Well, I can promise you we didn't make him up."

Robinson remained surly. "Might as well have, because he's long gone. Now I'm willing to let you stay in London for your talk, but you don't go anywhere else but London. Then you get back here immediately after the talk's done. And don't give Special Agent Chambers a hard time." Wallie gave them a sweet smile. "She's a valuable asset, even when she's interfering with your business. I've worked with her in D.C., so I know what a hard-ass she can be." By then Wallie had stopped smiling. "That's why I've asked for her assistance. Understand what I'm telling you, Professor?"

"Ha!" Zelda raised a scrap of paper in triumph. "Raleigh. It's Raleigh."

"What is Raleigh?" Klewe asked.

"Told you I'm good at Scrabble." She flattened the crinkled sheet in front of Wallie and Klewe. On the page, one name of seven letters was written above another of equal length:

HAL IGER

RALEIGH

Klewe gave her an encouraging smile and then pretended to be upset. "Why couldn't you have figured that out two days ago?"

She patted him on the shoulder patronizingly. "Next I'll work on that little problem you have with Sonnet 55. Maybe I can solve that one for you too."

As they studied the paper with Iger's name, Wallie reached past Klewe to pick up the phone. "Eddie? It's the hard-ass again. Any particular business you want me to interfere with this time?"

Robinson decided to wait for the excited chatter in the background between Klewe and Zelda to subside.

"That marked G in the sonnet really raises some interesting questions." Zelda was commenting. "There must be a reason Shakespeare chose to shorten 'Against' that way."

"But why make that particular initial stand out? And then there's Raleigh to consider. Why the hell would someone toy with us this way?"

Klewe and Zelda fell silent for a moment.

"Finally," Detective Robinson said. "Hey, Wallie?"

"Yeah?"

"We'll be working with Interpol and the French police on this. In the meantime I need you to keep the professor there on a leash."

"Got it."

"Good luck. And Wallie?"

"Yeah?"

"Make it a short leash."

Chapter 38.

"FILTHY BIRDS," WALLIE Chambers sharply denounced a flock of pigeons swiftly encircling their feet. They had barely exited the cab that brought them from St. Pancras to Trafalgar Square when the flock formed. "Be careful not to drop food. You'll only encourage them."

Klewe watched as Zelda gyrated to glimpse Nelson's Column and the four bronze lions that guard it, but Wallie seemed generally unimpressed by the sights. Zelda asked her, "Have you been working in London long?"

"Not long," she said. "Why? Don't I sound British to you?"

"More Southern, I'd say."

"I was born and raised in North Carolina. Then I moved to D.C. after the police academy and worked with Detective Robinson. Have you met his son Kenneth yet?"

"No," Klewe said, "but he's mentioned him."

"That kid's a real charmer. Must be a freshman in high school by now."

They dodged sightseers as they crossed the square celebrating the 1805 British naval battle and headed toward St. Martin's Place. Mid-morning sunlight filtered through a layer of clouds, and Klewe found he was enjoying himself simply to be back in London.

"You're looking better," Zelda noted.

"I feel better. Maybe we can get through this in one piece after all. Once we talk with the people at the National Portrait Gallery, we might even figure out who's behind all of it."

They lingered at the edge of Trafalgar Square while Klewe reset his pocket watch to London time. Zelda noticed a sign pointing off toward the National Gallery. "Is that where we're going?"

Wallie shook her head. "That's the main art gallery. The National Portrait Gallery is the one next to it. Houses the portraits of royals and celebrities from British history." An Arabic woman with two small children in tow bumped against her and apologized as she hurried by them.

"It's practically the United Nations around here," Zelda remarked, looking at the ethnic mix of locals and visitors. "I've never been in London before, but it makes me wonder how prejudice could exist here."

"She said the same thing about Paris," Klewe noted good-naturedly.

"Maybe I did," Zelda said, "but we've been told the British have their own history of hate crimes. Have you seen much racism in London?"

Wallie considered for a moment. "Not nearly what there's been in American history, especially with organizations like the Ku Klux Klan. I was just reading the autobiography of a U.S. Senator who once led a Klan chapter, long before he repudiated his membership."

"You mean Robert Byrd from West Virginia?" Zelda wondered, and Wallie nodded. "That's my home state. Until his death a few years ago, Byrd served longer in the U.S. Senate than anyone else."

"See?" Wallie asked. "Britain can't touch that for brazenness."

"Oh, I seem to recall Prince Harry raising quite a few eyebrows awhile back when he showed up for a costume party dressed in a Nazi uniform." Klewe paused to consider. "And I heard they've had to keep British fans from attending the World Cup in Germany for fear of their bad behavior toward the Germans."

"I guess prejudice is everywhere," Wallie agreed. "That's what makes it so hard to overcome. Like the terrorist attack on the subways and buses here back in the summer of 2005. You never expect it's coming, so how do you stop it?"

They bypassed the massive National Gallery and continued until they found themselves catercornered to the National Portrait Gallery. Wallie gestured for them to stop near the stone building, and the two moved in closer to hear her instructions. She began lecturing Klewe in particular.

"Listen up," she said, "I'm trusting you to stay with me today. But in case we should get separated for any reason, let's arrange something now. Where should we meet? Choose some place that's very public and easy for you two to find."

Klewe's eyes darted about to the neighboring buildings, but he wanted to identify an unmistakable landmark. "Let's say Westminster Abbey. There's a bust of Shakespeare in Poets' Corner," he said, "and I want Zelda to see it. Why not meet next to Shakespeare?"

The others nodded their agreement.

"That's where I'll look for you if I need to. But bear in mind," Wallie added solemnly, "I may not be the only one looking for you."

They joined the line at the entrance to the National Portrait Gallery, which displays a veritable Facebook of British notables from Renaissance England to modern times. "In 2006," Klewe began his lecture even before their walk through the metal detectors at the front door, "they held a special display here highlighting the known images of Shakespeare. Some of those images are what I'm hoping we'll see today."

Inside the entry on the ground floor were assorted groups of students and foreigners listening to hushed commentary about the historical figures seen throughout the building, including the Victorians displayed on the gallery's first floor. While Klewe kept talking, he realized that Zelda was looking sideways at other exhibits and Wallie had her eyes on the bustling visitors.

"Is anybody paying attention to me?" he asked rhetorically, and Zelda motioned for him to be quiet inside the gallery.

As they rode up an impressive two-story escalator, they moved from the Victorian era into the presence of the Tudor portraits. A walk toward Room 4 led them directly to the work most significant to Klewe in the entire collection. Directly before them was the original Chandos portrait of William Shakespeare, the painting thought by many to have the highest degree of authenticity for the playwright's likeness.

He let the image sink in before continuing. "Most of the portraits here are classified either by their artists or by their sitters, the people who are posing. This painting is called the Chandos portrait, but it's not named for its sitter or artist. Instead, Chandos was one of the portrait's early owners."

Zelda almost gasped. "But is that really supposed to be Shakespeare? Because he looks so …"

Klewe said nothing, waiting for her to locate the precise adjective she was seeking to describe the sitter in this oil on canvas before them. At last the word came to her.

"Dark," she concluded.

Chapter 39.

"EXACTLY," KLEWE RESPONDED, turning from the portrait to Zelda and back. "Not much like the Droeshout engraving at all, is it? A lot more hair and a ring in his left earlobe." He paused when he looked at the hoop in Shakespeare's ear and thought sadly of Mason Everly's gold stud. "An important part of my theory is that scholars have often described him in this painting with adjectives like 'dark-skinned' or even 'swarthy.'"

"Then why are people trying so hard not to acknowledge what's in plain view? Is it really that hard to believe their eyes?"

Klewe gave Zelda a half-smile, and they stayed in place as Wallie walked on through the exhibits. "The critics think that all of the written references—'upstart crow' and 'sable tear' and 'tanned antiquity'—were metaphorical, referring to something other than skin color. And I'd be willing to say that a single one could be metaphor, maybe even two of them. But when all three surviving phrases about him refer to blackness, I think it's worthy of some consideration."

"Especially with this portrait of him."

"What I find equally compelling, though, are the facts that we know about him as a playwright."

"All I know is he wrote lots of plays, most of which I haven't read."

"Somewhere between 36 and 40 plays, according to most scholars. But what's more fascinating than the number he wrote is the percentage of those plays that contain some reference to a character being black or of another race. In the middle of a supposedly homogenous all-white society of Elizabethan London, more than 10 percent of Shakespeare's plays make some kind of racial reference. That to me is extraordinary."

"Which plays do you mean? I know about 'Othello,' of course. And there's 'Antony and Cleopatra' with the Egyptian queen."

"Yes, historians are still debating it, but nobody can identify how dark Cleopatra's skin color was, much less Shakespeare's. Some say Elizabethans knew so little about foreigners that they couldn't differentiate between blacks and Moors. For his audience, Shakespeare would sometimes describe characters as 'black Moors' or even 'blackamoors,' like the musicians in 'Love's Labor's Lost.' And there's still debate about whether Othello himself was of dark Moorish ancestry or truly black." He stopped himself. "Just think how amazing Othello and Cleopatra are. They aren't merely characters in his work. They're the main characters in their plays. And then there is Shakespeare's first tragedy, Are you at all familiar with 'Titus Andronicus'?"

"Sorry," Zelda answered, looking like a student who had lost her homework.

"Don't be. Most critics dismiss it as an early play, a failure even, hardly worth a mention. But if you read the play carefully, you'll find something Elizabethans rarely saw. It features a major character who's black. A villain named Aaron the Moor."

"A villain?"

"Yes, a dastardly character, or so it seems, who has witnessed his own land being ransacked and his family murdered by the invading Romans. He comes back to Rome with them, where they want to murder his illegitimate child by a white woman. And he has the temerity to refuse to let that happen. He insists his biracial son deserves to live and even hides the infant with another couple to protect the boy's life."

"That doesn't sound very villainous to me."

"Now you're getting it. Think this through. A young William Shakespeare comes to London to prove himself as a playwright and an actor. For his first tragedy, he writes a huge part for a young black man to play. It's not the lead, because there would be actors in the company vying for the leads. But Aaron is a memorable character, and if Shakespeare's skin happens to appear a little bit darker than the other actors, so much the better to launch his acting career."

"That would definitely have helped him as a new player."

"There's been speculation that Aaron was among Shakespeare's first acting roles when he came to London. And we have a contemporary drawing of the 'Titus Andronicus' cast, showing several white characters and Aaron clearly depicted as a black man."

Zelda raised an eyebrow. "Maybe that's the most accurate drawing there is of Shakespeare during his lifetime." As she spoke, she felt Wallie tap her on the shoulder.

"We have to be moving along," Wallie said, checking her wristwatch. "If we're going to make our meeting."

"What meeting?" Klewe asked.

"I asked a Yard contact to pull a few strings for us. They're expecting us in a curator's office. I figured that's where Professor Everly would have gone to do his research."

His last research, Klewe thought sadly. As he followed Wallie and Zelda, he began to feel uneasy again.

The three were directed by a guard toward a small elevator at the end of a carpetless corridor. Wallie Chambers pressed a button for the next floor, and in a moment the door opened onto another long hall. In the middle of that hallway sat a stern-looking young woman with a sweeping head of hair cast in tight reddish ringlets. From her desk she gave the would-be intruders a look calculated to halt their progress.

"You must be Ms. Bristol," Wallie said, introducing herself and the two American visitors. The young woman yielded no more approbation than a blink of her eyes. "We are here to meet with Mr. Taliaferro."

Klewe and Zelda noticed the telephone button was labeled "Taliaferro," but Wallie had properly pronounced it "Toliver," and the young woman nodded. She efficiently checked the appointment book in front of her and lifted the desktop phone to her ear. "Mr. Taliaferro, your 10:15 is here to see you."

The way she rolled her eyes after hanging up almost made Wallie laugh. "Difficult boss?"

"Oh, you have one of those too?"

"I used to. Yours ever call you a hard-ass?"

"He'd better not," the young woman responded lightly, "but my wife does." With a fleeting grin at Wallie, she rose from behind the desk to point their way.

One of a dozen doors farther along the hallway opened, and a short wiry man in a pinstripe suit appeared. As he came closer, he occasionally placed a hand cautiously atop his salt-and-pepper comb-over to check whether the hair had accidentally shifted. Equally as brusque as his gatekeeper, whom he referred to as Jennifer, the assistant curator then informed the visitors, "I can't give you more than a few minutes." He eyed the overhead clock as he said it, clearly indicating that their few minutes had already begun.

The man preceded them down the hall to a doorway marked "George Taliaferro, Assistant Curator, Renaissance Art." His office, not much larger than a cubicle, provided an efficiently if not imaginatively furnished meeting space complete with a large hanging lamp focused above a central reading table.

"You may thank Special Agent Chambers here," the assistant curator starkly informed Klewe and Zelda in a less-than-welcoming tone, "for arranging this interview for you. We normally do not accommodate requests on such short notice."

"I do apologize," Klewe began, "but we are urgently trying to learn whatever you can tell us about my colleague, Professor Mason Everly. We believe he was here this past week to research portraits of Shakespeare. He would have been particularly interested in anything drawn during the playwright's lifetime or soon after his death in 1616."

Taliaferro acknowledged Klewe's request with a slight nod but no smile. "Your colleague indeed was here, and I have asked my staff to assemble for you the images that we know Professor Everly examined from our collection. You must realize, of course, that hundreds of paintings have had the claim made of being Shakespeare's likeness, but in reality there are no images of the playwright known for a certainty to have been drawn from life. I must wonder, however, why you would need to replicate Professor Everly's research when it was done so recently."

Before they had a chance to reveal Everly's death, there was a sharp knock at the door, and the businesslike gatekeeper slipped into the room carrying an armful of research materials. At Jennifer Bristol's entrance, the assistant curator again checked the wall clock and excused himself before leaving the room.

His assistant stacked the load of books and photocopies onto the central reading desk in front of them and divided the materials into two stacks, pictures of Shakespeare from the decades immediately after his death and those from later in the 17th and 18th centuries. The first pile was by far the shorter.

"The dating on these," she intoned with the formality of a docent, "is not meant to imply that the artist ever met William

Shakespeare, but at least these have been suggested by some to be actual portraits of him. Is there anything else you might require?" She was already backing toward the office door. "If you do need me, I shall be at my desk."

"Jennifer, is it?" Zelda inquired crisply. "I know you must have spoken with Mason Everly when he came to visit."

The assistant pushed a pair of reading glasses squarely against her face and seemed unnerved by such a personal inquiry. "Why, yes. The two of us did speak the other day."

"I didn't know him," Zelda continued, "but Professor Klewe tells me he was a very fine person."

"Was? Did something happen?"

"He's dead."

Jennifer remained stoic at the news. If she were even vaguely taken aback, it was a self-contained response. "I see," she finally said.

"That's why we've come. We're trying to find out what happened while he was in London this week. Can you think of anybody we should speak with about him?"

Tossing back the ringlets of red hair, the young woman pondered the question a short while. "I believe Mr. Allenby talked with him at great length."

"Who is that?"

"Mr. Allenby? He's a book publisher. A bit off-center, you might say, but nice enough. He makes very generous donations to fund art exhibits and acquisitions for the Renaissance collection, so he has his own research space down the hall. He may know something more."

Wallie, who had been browsing intently through the stacked materials in Taliaferro's office, turned toward the assistant. "Would you please see if we might have a word with him?"

Jennifer Bristol nodded and quickly left the room.

"We'll have to thank her for all this assistance," Klewe said, wading through the piles of research, but Zelda scoffed at the sentiment. "What? Don't you think it was nice?"

"I think it was odd."

"That she's helping us?"

"No." Zelda stared after her. "That she never even asked me how Mason died."

Chapter 40.

"DO COME IN," Ed Allenby invited the three visitors. The publisher, stocky and affable in his late 50's, stood inside the doorway of a private office at the National Portrait Gallery and adjusted the sleeves of his double-breasted tweed jacket. Retreating to an elaborate roll-top desk, he focused light blue eyes on Zelda as he glad-handed each one of them in turn. As soon as he started speaking, they'd noted the trace of an Australian accent in his speech.

He motioned for Zelda to take the comfortable chair behind the desk and offered two folding chairs to Klewe and Wallie.

"I publish books about artists and writers," Allenby confirmed, slicking back his short brown hair. "As Ms. Bristol probably told you, I spend too much of my time getting in the way here, but I've always found their portraits to be most revealing. And if you happen to be wealthy and eccentric enough to donate to the right causes, they allow you to keep a small research office here as well."

Behind him on the desk was a grainy photograph of Sir Edmund Hillary from the Mount Everest ascent. From beside the picture, Allenby picked up a shiny letter opener that he began to drum mindlessly onto a volume in front of him.

Wallie pointed to the photograph. "Are you eccentric enough to count that among your hobbies?"

The publisher coughed a loud, bursting laugh. "Scaling mountaintops? No, not at all. I was named for Hillary, but I've never had the courage to climb Everest myself. Would you?"

They each dismissed the idea, before Zelda poked Klewe in the arm and indicated the letter opener in Allenby's hand. When he looked more closely, he realized the opener was long and sharp, a silver replica of an Elizabethan dagger. It included a family crest engraved into the handle with the name "Gloucester" along the base.

"That thing looks dangerous," Zelda explained at Allenby's questioning glance.

"This? Only to envelopes." He dropped the letter opener into a desk drawer and turned back to them.

Klewe leaned forward in his chair. "We don't mean to interrupt your research. Perhaps Mr. Taliaferro or Ms. Bristol has told you we're looking for information about Professor Mason Everly, whom I believe you spoke with a few days ago."

Allenby nodded. "Yes, I do remember the gentleman. Proposed a wonderfully exotic theory about William Shakespeare, as I recall. I'll be publishing my own book on Shakespeare next year, so naturally we started chatting." He stopped and thought for a second. "Yes, I remember congratulating him on this new take on the Bard. I asked him to consider allowing me to publish your book when it was ready."

Klewe let out a gentle sigh of exasperation. "We're not close to that point."

"Still, you must admit it would be an idea of vast commercial appeal. People are always hungering for a new view of Shakespeare or for yet another conspiracy theory about history, and this book would certainly fill both those niche markets. Quite nicely, in fact."

"There is no book yet," Klewe emphasized again. "And, in case Ms. Bristol failed to inform you, my colleague was murdered the other night in Washington."

"Murdered?" Allenby's eyes opened wide. "She just told me that he had died. Most unfortunate, but I'm afraid I have little knowledge of where or what he was doing while he was here. Beyond researching your theory, of course."

Zelda asked the publisher, "Is it truly that commercial an idea? I wouldn't think racism back in Shakespeare's day would be such a hot topic now."

"Oh, my dear, the brutality of racism goes far back in Western culture. Scottish warriors were known to paint their bodies a dark blue before going into battle simply to strike fear into their opponents. And by Elizabethan times, the ugly notion of white as good and black as evil was rampant. One of Shakespeare's contemporaries, in fact, was a playwright named John Webster. He wrote 'The White Devil,' a popular drama with a title that played against the widespread notion that the devil himself was black. In fact, that title suggested how strange it would be for a devil to be white."

Allenby walked across to a low-hanging shelf of books in his office.

"I understand Ms. Bristol has assembled materials for you in the other office, but I have more here if you are interested." He indicated a lengthy row of shelved volumes. "To the best of my knowledge, there is simply no existing picture of Shakespeare drawn or painted during his lifetime by any artist who had seen him personally. That's why you'll find handsome Shakespeares and plain Shakespeares, some with little facial hair, some heavily bearded. A few show him with an earring or perhaps a ribbon dangling from his ear." He took hold of several books and scattered them before his listeners. "The National Portrait Gallery has even gone so far as to X-ray the paintings they have of him to search for earlier or trace paintings underneath them, but so far nothing has emerged that has any degree of authenticity."

He put up his hands in futility before he went on.

"I wish we knew more so we could tell you more. The books devoted to how Shakespeare looked are almost completely speculation. Some experts choose to discount a portrait, for instance, if his hair is black instead of auburn. As if we knew whether Shakespeare had any hair at all. Then there are the many forgeries and false images. Those will be featured in my new book, 'The Many Faces of Shakespeare.'"

"That was the main question Mason came here to investigate," Klewe told him. "Whether there were any reliable contemporary pictures of Shakespeare."

"And the answer is an unequivocal no. Not any of the paintings or any death mask. Not even the Stratford bust near his tomb, a bust that's been redone at least once. It was made by a Dutchman named Janssen after Shakespeare's death and later repainted, ostensibly to revive the original coloring after a whitewashing, but—"

"Perhaps to change the skin color?" Zelda speculated.

"They said at the time the repainting was to make it more lifelike, but who knows what the true motives were?"

"Even today," Klewe noted ruefully, "we've run into problems trying to determine people's motives."

"I can imagine how hard it must be to read the Elizabethan mind," Wallie said. "And you say you showed all this to Professor Everly while he was in London?"

Allenby nodded gravely.

"Then," Klewe asked him, "you can tell us of no artwork contemporary with Shakespeare that contradicts our theory?"

"Nothing at all, and I've been looking into that very question myself. Provocative stuff, but nothing definitive."

"I've been told that Mason planned to meet somebody, perhaps another historian, at the Globe today at noon. Somebody named Earl?"

"That would be Earl Wrist, I expect. A local scholar of Elizabethan and Jacobean drama. For the past few years, he has worked from a warehouse office in Southwark, but he spends a fair amount of his time at the Globe doing research."

"Earl Wrist, you say?"

Allenby nodded. "I'd try the Globe's bookstore. That's his favorite haunt."

A quick rap at the door was followed by Jennifer Bristol's appearance to say she had assembled the remaining materials for their perusal. She left the room as quickly as she had entered.

"If I do recall anything else," Allenby said, "I'll be certain to let you know." He lifted his coat from a hook beside the door. "But right now I must get to a meeting, if you'll excuse me. The best of luck with your work. And it's a shame, a terrible shame, about your friend. I hope you're able to find the answers you're seeking."

He was almost out the door when Zelda blocked his way with a final question. "We can't seem to find a reference from Shakespeare's time to explain some initials that were being used back then. Does 'G.S.' mean anything to you?"

"Sorry, no," he called as he hurried past the reception desk to the elevator. "I can't help you with that."

Wallie told them she wanted to walk out with Allenby. After informing Klewe she would be outside the gallery's main entrance, she rushed after the departing publisher.

Jennifer Bristol was back at her desk alphabetizing files when Klewe and Zelda finished sorting through the research. They had briefly overheard George Taliaferro's raised voice as he shouted a series of short commands at his assistant.

"You must have a difficult job," Zelda sympathized as they approached the younger woman's desk.

"You have no idea," Jennifer said softly.

"I'll bet Mason Everly appreciated your input when he was here." Zelda decided to pursue a hunch. "I imagine he asked you about that 'G.S.' business."

"Oh, that," the gatekeeper smiled. "Yes, I told him all about that. I remember how genuinely surprised he was. He never knew those letters stood for Shakespeare."

Chapter 41.

"WILLIAM SHAKESPEARE?" ASKED an incredulous Klewe. He had been listening in line behind Zelda, but he could not contain his curiosity.

"Of course," Jennifer Bristol responded indifferently.

He stepped around Zelda to take over the questioning. "How do you know that?"

"I told you," she said patiently, as though speaking to somebody particularly dense. "I'm trained as a Renaissance historian. Fine one I'd be if I didn't know Shakespeare's initials."

At that point Zelda rejoined the discussion. "But wouldn't they be 'W.S.' then? I mean, if it's supposed to be his initials?"

"I'm sure it was sometimes," Jennifer said, reacting uncomfortably when she noticed the time on the office clock. "There's a mountain of materials I need to collect for a telephone conference they're holding this afternoon." She rose to leave. "If you'll excuse me."

The dumbfounded pair moved in tandem and blocked her path from the desk. When she could tell they were adamant, she reseated herself and bent down, momentarily disappearing from view beneath the desktop. When her hands reappeared, she grasped a thick book that looked old and well-thumbed. Inspecting its spine, Klewe recognized it as a standard university collection of Shakespeare's plays.

"I have that edition," he told her as she sat upright again at the desk, "but I don't remember any 'G.S.' in there."

She smiled crookedly. "Perhaps you'll want to spend more time with the source material accompanying the plays." She opened the book to skim a table of contents for its illustrations and reproductions. With a speed reader's eye, she made her way quickly down the list to the exact item she sought and found a page number.

"Here," she said triumphantly. The large book whirled about in her hand and landed flat on the desk before them.

"What is it?" Zelda asked Klewe, who was busily studying the page and failed to answer.

"It's all right there," the young woman told them. "Haven't you ever seen his baptismal record?" She fingered a small photograph of Stratford's parish register recording a baptism in April 1564, along with the Shakespeare infant's given name. "Gulielmus."

"My God," he stammered. "She's right. The Latin name. William in Latin begins with a G, not a W. How could I forget that?"

"And that's the name in Shakespeare's birth record?" asked Zelda, a note of confusion creeping into her voice.

"No," Jennifer corrected, "it's not in a birth record. We don't have anything like that. It's in a baptismal record."

"That's true," Klewe said, turning to Zelda. "There are no surviving records of Shakespeare's birth, only a baptismal record dated April 26, 1564."

"Hold on a minute," Zelda said to him. "I thought everybody's calendar lists his birthday as being on the 23rd of April, not the 26th. Right around Earth Day, isn't it?"

"Historians have found that in those days there was usually a three-day wait between a baby's birth and baptism. In Shakespeare's case, we know from the official record that he was baptized on the 26th of April, so his birthday has been generally assumed to be April 23rd."

"The same day on the calendar," Jennifer added, "for celebrating St. George, our patron saint who slew the dragon."

Klewe nodded his assent. "We're fairly sure that played heavily in the decision of which day to call Shakespeare's birthday."

"I don't know about this," Zelda said. She had pulled out her notebook and was scribbling hasty notes. "It seems a bit of a reach to me. Wasn't he known as William during his lifetime? Not by that name, whatever it was you said."

"It's Gulielmus," Jennifer repeated in a businesslike tone, "and it's not a name that just anybody would have associated with Shakespeare. It was Latin, the language of the truly educated." She looked at the motley pair before her as though pig-Latin were more their style. "It was the way he would have been known by other serious writers of his time. Here, just a minute."

She took yet another dive beneath her desk to what Klewe now began to imagine must be an entire library of reference works hidden under there. A moment's rustling sound, followed by a slight grunt, allowed her to produce an even larger volume, this one making a pronounced thud as it came down on the wooden surface of the desk.

The volume covered a range of English Renaissance poetry, and with her usual efficiency Jennifer turned pages rapidly to scour a list of entries at the back of the book. When the index revealed what she wanted, she flipped briskly to the desired page, again spinning the book to show the others.

"The poetry of John Weever," Klewe said. "I remember reading that back in grad school, but it's been a few years."

"I can imagine," Jennifer said, but she gave no indication that she meant the comment as a slight. Instead, she sighed to suggest that this exercise in literary history was exhausting her daily supply of research hours. "Latin was popular back then as the preferred language to be used among the literati."

With Zelda breathing heavily over his shoulder, Klewe ran his finger down the page until he came upon Weever's sonnet to a contemporary poet. It was a tribute poem, dating back to 1599, and began with a reference to "Honey-tongued Shakespeare." Under Jennifer's tapping finger, the title of the poem almost popped off the page: "Ad Gulielmum Shakespeare."

"Spelled a bit differently, but it's still William. Anything else?" Jennifer asked. They shook their heads and thanked her before she gathered up a stack of files and disappeared down the hallway in the opposite direction from their elevator.

"There it is," Klewe said. "It's been right there in front of me all this time."

"Who would have thought to use G for an abbreviation of William?" Zelda worried she might need to console him, but his scholarly passion had clearly overwhelmed any need for consolation.

"Shakespeare would, that's who. I'll bet that's why he marked the G with an apostrophe, to show it was being altered. Ingenious." He looked from the one book to the other, an excitement rising in his voice as he spoke. "It's truly ingenious. And it's all right there in Sonnet 55. 'G.S.' stands for William Shakespeare, along with the words 'Ebony Swan.' Sonnet 55 has it all, encoded to keep the School of Night or White Crow or anybody else from ever being able to destroy it or to cover up the truth."

She stood there watching him in silence.

"Mason kept telling me it was out there somewhere. I'm so glad that he was able to find it before ..."

"Do you suppose that's why he came back to D.C. so suddenly?" Zelda wondered.

"I don't know. He used N35 to pinpoint Holy Trinity Church, so maybe he was indicating the baptismal records in Stratford. Or there could be something more out there we still haven't found."

"Isn't this enough? For you to present the theory, I mean?"

"As much as we may ever have," he answered honestly. "And I really owe it to Mason to make the idea public. Tonight."

"So," Zelda said lightly, "now that you've saved the world, what should we do with the rest of our day in London? How about a walk?"

"Seriously?" Klewe's feet still ached from the long trek around Paris. "We need to find Wallie outside before we go anywhere."

"Then we can eat."

"Soon, but first I have to meet somebody at the Globe." He stopped shy of the elevator door and pondered, his eyes shining. "I wonder how many times Shakespeare said that."

Chapter 42.

"DON'T EVER TAKE up poker," Wallie Chambers advised the canary-swallowing twosome when they emerged from the National Portrait Gallery. While Zelda and Klewe busily explicated their new insights into the Sonnet 55 puzzle, she remained distant to their excitement, clearly thinking about something else.

Finally, Zelda asked, "What's the problem?"

"No problem. I talked some more with that Allenby character. He told me he knows nothing about a cell called White Crow."

"But you don't believe him?"

"No, I don't. I get the feeling he knows a lot more than he claims."

Zelda contemplated the possibility and said, "That's what Chris tells me. People know more than they say."

"That's true. Anyway," Wallie continued, "I was just calling Scotland Yard. I had been scheduled to meet with a C.I. there this morning, and he was not thrilled that I'm spending the entire day with you." The two vehemently denied needing her services as a sitter, but she ignored their protests. "I did ask the Chief Inspector about White Crow. As far as he knows, there's been no new intel chatter. But he also said there's always some Aryan or neo-Nazi foolishness being intercepted." She placed her phone back into her trenchcoat pocket. "It may mean these people live off the grid, which makes it almost impossible to find them. Until they've done something." She hoped the last part would make a profound impact on the listeners, and it did.

After a momentary silence, Klewe meekly observed, "I guess we should be grateful we're in London and it's not raining today."

"I can see you came prepared," Wallie said.

"This?" He held up the closed umbrella. "You have no idea how useful this thing has been."

"Does he still wear those god-awful sweaters?" she asked Zelda, who sized him up carefully.

"I don't know," she admitted. "But it does seem a little chillier here than it was in Paris." With a flourish, Zelda unfolded her scarf with gold and burgundy stripes. Wrapping it around her neck, she wasn't expecting her move to elicit a thumbs-up signal from Wallie.

"Go, Washington! The team colors, right?"

"I thought you didn't have much NFL over here."

"Not much, but I lived in D.C. for years. Besides," Wallie said, leveling a serious stare at them, "real fans never forget football."

"Well, forget it today," Zelda said. "I've never been to London. Who wants to show me the sights? And I'll need to buy a sweatshirt for my collection."

"Aren't your feet worn out from Paris?" Klewe hobbled his way toward a lamppost for a chance to lean against it. "There must be a Tube station near here."

"Come on," Zelda prodded him. "You can't see anything from the Underground."

"How about an organized walk?" Wallie suggested in compromise. "They don't take long. All you do is show up and pay the tour guide."

"How many places can we see in one day? So far you've promised me Poets' Corner at Westminster Abbey. And the Globe, of course. Where else?"

Klewe mouthed the words "Help me" in Wallie's direction, but to no discernible advantage.

"Depends on the tour," Wallie answered her. "Different ones cover different parts of London, from ghost walks to Jack the Ripper crime scenes. I do know of one starting soon that I think you'll like." She glanced at her watch. "And the line for it is usually forming about this time."

The three of them strolled to the station at Charing Cross, where they found a short line forming near the subway's street-level entrance. An effusively happy woman wearing a long checked dress and a plaid beret was raising a small orange flag above her head while she busily semaphored together a group of sightseers. She had already started to collect her fee from a dozen customers as she advertised her "walk and ride" tour of the Embankment and surrounding areas.

"Where will you be taking us?" Zelda asked the guide.

The woman surveyed them briskly and cheerily replied, "We walk the very same steps Shakespeare did during the reign of our first Elizabeth."

Klewe wondered how anyone could possibly know where Shakespeare had walked four centuries ago, but there was another topic that concerned him far more. "And what do we mean by 'walk and ride'?"

"Oh, that," the guide said. "We walk both sides of the Thames. After our initial session here, we travel to the South Bank to continue the tour. But don't be concerned. That part is already included in our cost."

"What part?"

"Why, our boat ride across the river," she explained enthusi-astically. "You and your friends will love it. We reach the Globe by half past noon."

Klewe could already feel the blood draining from his face. "I don't think so," he told Zelda and Wallie, motioning for them to go on without him.

"He has a thing about rivers," Zelda started to explain.

"I remember that," Wallie said, looking sympathetically at him.

"You two take the tour," he suggested. "I'll meet you on the South Bank when you get there."

"Are you certain?" Zelda said, fully anticipating his answer.

"Yes. I'll cross over by bridge and meet Earl Wrist at the Globe. By that time, your boat should have docked there."

Wallie, however, eyeballed Klewe like a stray animal under her supervision. "I'm not to let you out of my sight. Even if that means we all stay together."

Klewe tried to dissuade her. "You two go. I can take care of myself." When he saw Zelda's expression, he quickly added, "Not that Zelda can't."

"You're the one they're after, aren't you?" Wallie reasoned. "Zelda can take the tour alone, while I shadow you and make sure everything goes well at your meeting."

When Zelda reminded Klewe she had no British money, he counted out notes from the currency Wallie had exchanged for him at the train station.

"And take this," he said to Zelda confidentially, pulling out the clover to hand her. "I'm told it's good luck." He stood next to Wallie and watched until the walking tour had rounded a far cor-ner. He kept watching, not feeling right, even after Zelda was no longer in sight.

Then Klewe allowed Wallie to direct their walk toward the noon meeting. Before he realized it, they were already nearing the Thames.

"Let's go," she said, but he froze in place, shaking his head resolutely.

"Not me," he said as he warily eyed the latest addition to London bridges. Ahead of them stretched a metallic footbridge known as the Millennium Bridge. It did provide the fastest way to cross, but it was also an open-air adventure, daunting for anybody worried about the water below.

No sooner had he proposed the Southwark Bridge as an alternative than his watcher agreed and turned left toward it. The Southwark was a far older and more substantial bridge of green and yellow, designed for cars as well as pedestrians and far less exposed to a river view.

"We're lucky to have a choice of bridges," Wallie said to him. "When your man Shakespeare lived here, they had to go by boat or pay for the privilege to cross a bridge. Or, in the winters, they could walk across the river when it froze."

"I've seen that mural of the frozen Thames with people crossing over it, but I wouldn't have tried."

"Me neither." Wallie was suddenly besieged by several black-birds gathered on the bridge. With a swift kick of her leg, she scattered them wildly. "Never have cared much for birds."

"Why's that?"

"Superstitions, I guess."

"But don't they say England will last until the ravens leave the Tower of London?"

"Yup, where they cut off Sir Walter Raleigh's head. They also say that if a raven lands on your house, it means death for someone inside, but that may come from mistaking its call for the word 'corpse.' I do know birds can be dangerous. Cousins of mine in Texas told me a few years ago that, for no apparent reason, a flock of grackles attacked people in downtown Houston. How about that?"

They had almost completed their walk across the bridge. Klewe was only half listening, his eyes straight ahead to avoid looking down at the rippled surface of the Thames. Instead, he focused on the approaching bank, his gaze drawn inevitably off to the west and the London Eye, a giant Ferris wheel erected at the Millennium. At length he allowed himself to scan part of the river ahead, because he wanted a clear view of his single most favorite London sight. And there it stood as if waiting for him on the South Bank.

The great Globe itself.

Chapter 43.

THE RECONSTRUCTED GLOBE Theater, a breath-
taking mix of oak and thatch and handmade bricks, loomed large at
the southern edge of the Thames, the building's almost rounded
design magnificent in the late morning sun.

Klewe had experienced mixed feelings when he'd first heard
years earlier of efforts to recreate the great theater. Its builders,
however, had stayed painstakingly faithful to the original construction, at least as much as was known about it, down to using authentic building materials and construction practices from the
Renaissance.

By early November, the Globe's theater season had already
come to a close for the winter months, but the open-topped
structure still drew tourists and drama students like a magnet. In his
previous visits, Klewe had enjoyed standing just inside the entrance
of the replicated theater and watching visitors be enthralled by the
spectacle. This time, though, his thoughts were centered on the
evening's talk he was to give in one of the Globe's indoor lecture
rooms.

He and Wallie made their way up a long ramp inside the co-
lossal structure. Once they reached the gift shop, they separated
briefly to ask the store's clerks whether they knew of an Earl Wrist.

The two met up again beside a display of London maps and Shakespeare coffee mugs.

"Any luck?" Wallie asked.

"Not yet. Nobody seems to know him. If there even is an Earl Wrist to be found."

At that moment, from behind him, a bald middle-aged man in an off-white suit tapped his shoulder and inquired, "Are you looking for me?" They turned to see him tightening his grip on a white woolen scarf wrapped about his neck.

"Professor Wrist?"

"Mister Wrist would be more accurate. I'm a scholar, not a teacher."

"I was told you might be here," Klewe said.

"Why were you looking for me?" the older man questioned him in a hushed voice. Appearing somewhat skittish, he wore brown-framed glasses with thick lenses and nervously ran a hand repeatedly over his completely clean-shaven head.

Gesturing that Wallie should maintain her distance, Klewe bent forward and began to speak confidentially. "Please excuse this intrusion. I'm Christopher Klewe, a professor from the United States. I believe you had a meeting planned today with a colleague of mine, Mason Everly."

"Yes," Wrist said, staring down owlishly at a small wristwatch on a wide band. "Edmund Allenby called me the other day and asked me to meet with Professor Everly. I understand he's to give a lecture here this evening." He looked about uncertainly and began to clear his throat. It led him into a coughing fit, which seemed to quell only after he tied the scarf more tightly about his neck. "I thought you might be the gentleman. Is he here with you?"

"No, I'm afraid not. Something happened."

The older man wasn't surprised. "He's dead, isn't he?"

"How did you know?" Klewe asked, then nodded gently. "He's been murdered. Any idea why he wanted to see you?"

"I'd agreed to help him," Wrist said stoically. "I shouldn't have." With that, he turned back to a long counter of Shakespeare merchandise and feigned interest in the price tags.

"Are you afraid?" Klewe wondered. "Is it White Crow?"

Wrist quieted him anxiously and surveyed the area again to see who might be watching. "Yes, I am afraid. Shouldn't you be as well?"

"Not enough to let them stop me. I've already called the Globe sponsor to arrange for me to make the speech in place of my colleague. If you were going to help Mason, can't you help me now?"

"I've done what I can. I was going to tell your friend his theory about Shakespeare is not just flawed. It's completely wrong."

"How so?"

"My good man, I have been a scholar of Elizabethan England my entire life. What you're saying they meant by 'black' back then is incorrect. That word was used in many ways. Hamlet, for instance, is sometimes known as 'the black prince.' It could be a coloring of one's mood or one's hair or even one's dress. Did you know that the Puritan leader who counseled Elizabeth the First was known as her 'little black husband' solely because he wore a dark robe?"

"I do know that, but I also know that he was never referred to as an 'upstart crow,' nor did anybody bother to apologize to him in print for what he was called."

"Listen," Wrist said, choking again into his scarf, "I only came here today as a courtesy to warn your colleague not to make his talk. It's good advice, and you should heed it as well. If you'll excuse me."

Wrist started to walk away, but Wallie stepped up to block his path. "What more can you tell us about White Crow?" she demanded of the timid scholar, who acted stunned that somebody else had accompanied Klewe to the Globe.

"This is a friend of mine," Klewe explained to him, "and we need to know everything you can tell us about that group."

"I cannot say more," he said, twisting back and forth to check for signs of impending trouble. "I must get back to my office."

"Mason Everly sent me a final text the day he died. Does the phrase 'my bones' mean anything special to you?"

"It does," the older man responded to Klewe without blinking. "It means something special to every last one of us."

"And what's that?"

He gave a small shrug. "Death," he said.

Chapter 44.

EARL WRIST WAS clearly finished with their encounter and turned abruptly to make his exit from the Globe. Klewe hastened his own pace to intercept the scholar on the sidewalk outside. "I still don't know why Professor Everly wanted to see you," he said, signaling Wallie again to keep her distance.

"We are all seeking answers about Shakespeare in our own ways," Wrist replied as they strolled along. "I too have gone to the National Portrait Gallery to study the images. I wanted to see what religious symbols I might find. Was Shakespeare Protestant? Or was he a secret Catholic? Perhaps something else. He's been identified at various times as Jewish, atheist or pagan. We can never be sure what the right answer is, and our perspectives change over time. Take a look over there." He pointed out a tall structure along the edge of the road ahead. "What does that look like to you?"

Klewe checked discreetly first to ensure Wallie was still following them. They had left the Globe behind and were crossing a wide road into an area featuring the redevelopment of old shops and Southwark warehouses.

"An office building, I suppose. Or an apartment house."

"Rose Tower. It's made most lists of 'the weirdest sights in London,' as an office development atop an archeological dig. This is Rose Alley that runs along here, and you'd never suspect that what you are seeing was once the Rose Theater, one of the most important of Elizabethan England's playhouses. But the Rose wasn't used only as a stage. It was sometimes a brothel, sometimes a ring for bloody animal fights. A very dangerous place. Now it's a blue-plaque historic site for tourists to ogle."

Klewe was tempted to take a longer look at it himself, but Wrist kept walking. He led the way to a shaded alleyway and stopped at a warehouse with no signage out front.

"We are told that some of Shakespeare's early plays were staged there in the Rose, but we cannot know for sure. In fact, there are many things we cannot know for certain. Where Shakespeare is concerned, my dear Professor Klewe, there are always going to be more questions than answers."

"Does that mean legitimate questions should not be raised out of reluctance or ignorance or fear?"

"I will argue with you no more," Wrist concluded. "I have done all I can to warn you."

The men stood facing off at the entrance to the long warehouse. The building appeared to Klewe to be deserted, but Wrist unlocked its main door and went inside.

"Warn me about what?"

The older man began to shut the door in his face. "White Crow."

Instinctively, Klewe blocked the front door with his foot. "What about White Crow?"

"You must know something about them," Wallie addressed him, stepping forward from the shadows.

"I thought at first they were something out of myth," the scholar admitted. "Their name sounded a bit like some native tribe. From what I've read of your American Indians, they've recognized the crow or raven as a trickster, capable of turning itself into something else. Not unlike those Transformer toys children play with."

"But now," Klewe encouraged him, "you know this group isn't just playing. What can you tell us about them?"

"Let us say I know what White Crow is capable of doing."

"Are they part of the School of Night?"

Wrist refused to meet his stare. "A splinter cell, from what I hear, far more sinister than the parent group. Do not cross them."

From the outside, they tried to gain entry to the warehouse, but Wrist adamantly rebuffed their efforts to advance. He shoved Klewe away from the front door. When Wallie moved closer to protect him, Klewe waved at her to stay back.

"What more can you tell us about their activities?" Klewe implored.

"When you ask me about White Crow, what you may not know is that crows are among the smartest of all birds. Do not underestimate them." He tilted his head, carefully evaluating Klewe. "You think you are smart and have it all figured out, the way the whole world should be. But not everybody in the world agrees with you. You refer to others as racists? The fact is there has never been a human society that did not have some type of racism intrinsically built into it. And every society, my friend, believes itself to be the ideal. Some native tribes even developed their own mythology about race. Are you familiar, for instance, with a creation myth based on baking?"

Klewe shook his head and waited for the older scholar to elucidate.

"In these racial myths, the tribal members believe the Great Maker created people by baking them. In a first attempt, the white man came out underdone, so the Maker was forced to try again. Then the black man came out seemingly burned. On the Maker's third try, though, the perfect human turned out to be brown. Is that not racist in its own way?"

Klewe bristled, having heard enough. "Other groups are racist, so that permits you to promote hatred and bigotry? That's what you think makes a suitable society?"

"I am not alone, Professor. I have traveled far in my lifetime, and I have heard many ideas you would not be willing to entertain, much less share. Should that spreading of knowledge be tolerated?"

"We tolerate a great many things we don't like. That doesn't mean people accept those notions."

"I don't know how to make the warning any clearer," Wrist said, taking hold of Klewe's right arm. "Whatever else you may believe, these people are not simpletons. In fact, they already know about you and your wife." His eyes flashed over at Wallie. "And your watchdog here too, I would imagine."

When Wrist released his arm, Klewe backed off. Wallie thought he might be planning to lash out at the older man, but Klewe turned and bolted away from the warehouse. Wallie sprinted up the alleyway behind him.

"Slow down," she called to him. "Who cares that he thinks I'm helping you? I've been called worse than a watchdog before."

Over his shoulder, Klewe called back without breaking stride, "That's not the problem. It's Zelda."

"What about her?"

"I hadn't even mentioned her to him." He stopped briefly to catch his breath next to the Rose Theater archeological site on their way back to the Globe. "And there's only one other person I know who thinks she's my wife."

Chapter 45.

MOVING AT A steady clip, Klewe emerged with Wallie from the shadow of the Southwark warehouse into the early afternoon sunlight. They were heading back to the Globe Theater, where they skirted the massive exterior to come within sight of the boats that were docking on the southern edge of the Thames. With no hesitation whatsoever, Klewe aimed directly for the riverside. He ran to the dock reserved for tour boats, fearful of what he knew he would discover there.

Zelda was not aboard.

"Your friend's not with us," the bereted tour guide with the orange flag called out cheerfully from among the passengers. She remained in the middle of the boat offering the same vacuous smile to the tourists who had begun the organized walk on the northern side of the river.

"Where did she go?"

"Off with someone. A woman, I think," the guide said, failing to sound as jovial as she'd pretended. Then she frowned. "Maybe not. Our group was passing the Sherlock Holmes pub at the time, and I'm afraid my hands were full."

"It was a woman, you said," Wallie repeated, hoping to encourage further description.

"Maybe not," she reminded her, lifting the small flag to gather the walking group about her onto the Southwark bank. "She seemed to go willingly enough, and I simply cannot be expected—" The whine of her voice trailed away as Klewe and Wallie rushed from the dock.

"We need to find her." Klewe looked wildly about. "Now."

Wallie surveyed the riverfront and the Globe. "The taxi line's too long on this side. Let's go back across the river. We'll find her, or Detective Robinson will lop off my head like Raleigh's."

Winding her way between tourists and Londoners during the lunchtime rush, Wallie preceded Klewe toward Southwark Bridge. Instead of following her, though, Klewe dashed to his left and jumped determinedly onto the steel Millennium Bridge. Soon he was pushing his way through pedestrians on the low-slung suspension bridge, its framework open to see the wavy surface of the Thames.

"Wait up," Wallie called to him. Other pedestrians brushed against them, but within a few minutes they reached the northern bank in view of St. Paul's Cathedral. "Hey," she asked him after an inspired thought, "didn't we all agree to meet at Poets' Corner?"

Klewe followed her initiative, his adrenaline pumping. They sped along the northern bank of the Thames toward Westminster and the Houses of Parliament. Wallie knew the fastest approach to reach Westminster Abbey and, once they did, they headed through the crowded entryway in its enormous Gothic façade. Amid the commotion at the historic building's front door, a carefully groomed man in a guard's uniform cautioned them to slow down, and they asked his directions for finding Poets' Corner. He handed them a brochure and pinpointed the area for tombs and monuments in the South Transept devoted to the great British authors. The names of those celebrated formed a litany of literary giants— Chaucer, Milton, Keats, Dickens, even Oscar Wilde—as well as famous actors like David Garrick and the ashes of Lord Laurence

Olivier. Klewe marveled that Ben Jonson had been interred in the Abbey "standing upright" by his own request.

"I'm stunned Shakespeare wasn't buried here," Wallie was saying. "Almost all the big names from British history are in the Abbey, from Elizabeth the First to Cromwell. And don't forget Jonas Hanway."

"Who's that?"

"The first Londoner to use an umbrella." She pointed to the one Klewe still clutched tightly. They worked their way through the crowd of sightseers milling about the interior of the sanctuary. Zelda was not among them.

As they came up to the Shakespeare monument, they noticed how his figure seemed to overlook the rest of Poets' Corner. The statue showed Shakespeare standing with his legs crossed, his elbow resting on books and his fist pressed to his chin. When they looked down at the floor beneath him, they could see a sparkle of green paper. Klewe reached down breathlessly, recognizing it as a wrapper for Doublemint. When he lifted the paper, he found underneath it a small glass trinket containing a clover.

Nicely done, Zelda, Klewe said to himself, lifting her good-luck charm from the floor.

"What are you finding?" Wallie asked, bending beside the crouched figure of Klewe to inspect the area. He showed her the gum wrapper and the trinket.

"Zelda was here. I'm sure she dropped this wrapper for us to find."

"And what's that thing?"

Klewe didn't reply at first. He had stopped to consider what was about to happen. He knew Wallie was going to object to what he needed to do, so he rose to his full height and gave a dismissive shrug.

"It's her good-luck charm. I'm not sure, but I have an idea where I can find her."

"Oh, no, you don't. Not by yourself. In fact," Wallie said decisively, "I want to park you somewhere safe until your speech tonight, and I'll go looking for your friend. Just tell me what you're thinking."

"When she showed me this charm, she mentioned buying another one at a train station near Baker Street. Marylebone's the name, isn't it? I'm thinking we can find her there."

Reluctantly Wallie followed him from the Abbey and used her cell. "I'll have an associate meet us there who can watch out for you. Damn it, no answer." She hurried out to the street corner behind him, where they joined a short line for black cabs. "Don't try anything heroic," she warned Klewe officially, but he was busily plotting the surest way for a dog to slip its leash.

Chapter 46.

A VIEW OF Dutch gables atop Marylebone Station rose unexpectedly fast through the narrowed windows of their black cab. Klewe leapt out of the taxi and was already rushing inside the terminal of red brick and cream-colored stone before Wallie could finish paying their driver.

It was the lunch hour, and Klewe found himself roundly annoyed by the dense numbers of people scattered around the small shops and pub. He was even more upset by how closely his traveling companion had attached herself to him. Since Westminster Abbey, Wallie could not be shaken from his side. Now they raced together past the luggage carts and the assembled passengers in the terminal, only to come to a standstill before a giant board listing the arrivals and departures of diesel trains at the half-dozen platforms.

Wallie gave a low groan. "I don't see how a gum wrapper will help us with what's up there." She glared suspiciously at Klewe. "Are you sure she intended to come to this station?"

"I'm sure. Marylebone is where she said she wanted to come, but I can't tell you precisely why."

"Precision never seems all that important with you, I've noticed."

Klewe bristled. "What the hell is that supposed to mean?"

"You Bardophiles. From what I've heard, you can't even be certain when your man died."

"Sort of."

"That's an odd answer." They were being constantly jostled by riders eager to glean track numbers from the giant board. Out of the corner of her eye, Wallie spotted a coffee counter with small tables in the front. "Come on," she said, threading her way through the crowd and getting two cups of steaming coffee for them. "A year in London, and I still can't get used to drinking tea." When they had settled onto vinyl-covered seats, she handed him his cup and noticed his hands tremble as he lifted it. Lowering her voice, she asked gently, "Is the condition getting worse?" He nodded, unwilling to say more, so she changed the topic. "So what's this 'sort of' business about Shakespeare's death?"

"We know he died in 1616," Klewe began, his hands trembling as he lifted his cup, "but all we really have is a funeral record. That year he was laid to rest on April 25, so we assume he died a couple days before that. And since we think he was born on April 23, everybody likes to think he died at the age of 52 on the same date as his birthday. That's supposed to be a sign of genius, they say, being born and dying on the same calendar date."

"So the records aren't precise, just as I said."

"Maybe, but that's true of the majority of records from that time. They were no more exact for most of his contemporaries." He took a long swallow of coffee and balked at the strong liquid, pushing his cup away. "This isn't helping find Zelda, but thanks anyway. And I prefer tea."

"Slow down. I need my caffeine fix."

"Can we at least walk around the tracks? I'm hoping we'll see her."

Wallie relented and pushed aside her cup. They left the table and scurried back to the overhead sign of track assignments. Klewe read through the list of departures until he had memorized the one he would need.

He started alongside the first set of tracks, as Wallie followed doggedly at his heels. Then he moved along to the next train. The following platform had departing trains loading to either side. He stopped at each car, taking time to stare inside the darkened windows as if he were studying the face of each passenger already aboard.

"I'm thinking we should split up to cover these trains," he finally said to Wallie. "Also, they may be able to help us at the ticket window. Whoever took her would have needed to buy tickets."

Wallie shook her head. "Not necessarily. They could have purchased ahead. Or they can sometimes buy tickets on the train." She thought for a moment. "But it seems to me it would be way too risky to bring an unwilling passenger aboard a train. Let's wait for my guy to arrive, and he'll take you back to my office for safekeeping."

After hearing a loudspeaker's final call for the next departure, Klewe stopped short in his pacing. His mouth slacked open, and he pointed frantically to the line of passengers at the farthest ticket window.

"It's Zelda!"

Waving wildly in that direction, Klewe began running, knowing that Wallie would easily overtake him. Within seconds, Special Agent Chambers was the first to arrive at the ticket window. And within seconds after that, she knew she'd been had.

Behind her sounded the closing call for a departing train, and she retraced her steps to the platform. There was Klewe onboard, standing immediately inside the last car and holding up the umbrella he'd used to force his last-minute entry.

"Where did she go?" Wallie demanded through the closed door, but Klewe mimed that he was unable to hear. She pounded on the train window with her fist before shouting at him, "You can't go alone!" But it was her next question that caused his knees to weaken beneath him. "Could Zelda be in on it?"

Klewe stepped back as if he'd been struck viscerally. He shook his head violently, trying to rattle the idea loose. The train started chugging away, making Wallie shout even louder in her attempt to get through to him. She forced one final question through the closed door, imploring him to reconsider.

"How do you think," Wallie argued, "she got to Poets' Corner?"

THE FIFTH ACT:
EBONY SWAN

Chapter 47.

KLEWE STUMBLED BACKWARD into the main aisle of the train, still reeling from Wallie's parting shot. He staggered to the first empty seat along the aisle and collapsed into it.

Trying to calm himself, he listened to a rambling announcement that listed a stream of place names for the current run. The loudspeaker's static reverberated throughout the moving car, but he was satisfied when he found out he was aboard the correct train. He also knew it would not take Wallie long to determine his destination. He sat back heavily in the cushioned seat and gave a deep sigh.

On the afternoon train, the other passengers he saw were mostly locals bound for nearby shopping or business. When the conductor came along the aisle, Klewe counted out money for his passage. Behind the conductor was a small cart with squeaky wheels, a pudgy-faced vendor steering it. Klewe paid for a plastic-wrapped lunch of cream cheese sandwiches and a bottle of water. He downed the food quickly, not having realized how hungry he was, and then tried shutting his eyes in a fruitless effort to steel his nerves.

A woman in a cloth coat bumped him with a large briefcase when she climbed across him to the window seat. She tossed him an apologetic smile and became engrossed in the contents of her bag, while he went back to his own disturbing thoughts.

Wallie's last questions filled him with unease. Was it really possible that Zelda could be more than an observer in all this? That thought, as troubling as it was, led him into even more disturbing questions, and the more he considered them, the worse he felt.

What did he know about Zelda, really? How had she become so intensely linked with him, and so quickly? She alone had talked to Hal Iger outside Kennedy Center that first night. She alone had spotted the face of Shakespeare in the next car of the Metro train. She had separated from him outside the cabin before he found Amanda's body, and she had insisted on being left alone in Paris at the Ecole de Nuit.

And she had lied to him. Not once or twice since they met, but repeatedly and convincingly. She was not married, nor was she a Times reporter as she had originally represented herself. He was even beginning to wonder about that email to L15 and what might have happened to the other reporter that Mason Everly intended to inform of their research. Zelda's ambitions made her want a major news story, enough to manipulate the truth far too easily. Klewe fumbled inside his jacket pocket for the glass-covered clover, the one she claimed had come from Shakespeare's grave. And now, he thought as the train increased its speed toward the British countryside, Zelda had him lying to the authorities as well.

He'd been burned before, but he was struggling not to let himself believe the case against Zelda. In the last few days, she had faced some serious threats by being with him. He also knew, however, that he could easily end those threats by delivering his lecture at the Globe that evening. So why was he instead aboard a train heading out of London, putting himself in jeopardy to help find Zelda? And why had he felt justified in lying to Special Agent Chambers about it?

His thoughts focused on a multicultural Shakespeare, the bi-racial Bard he was planning to present to the world, and almost instantaneously he thought of "Othello." He had taught that Shakespearean tragedy enough times to know its warnings about listening to bad advice instead of heeding the one you value most. His mind envisioned the horrific scene where Othello smothers his wife in a jealous rage brought on by a traitorous friend. Klewe had made clear to his students that trusting the wrong person is what led to Othello's undoing. The solution to his own dilemma was now equally clear to him.

He believed Zelda. It was that simple. He had faith in her and could not imagine she was betraying him. Whatever he did not yet know about her, he knew she had earned his trust the last few days by showing tremendous courage, far more than he'd recognized. Diligently he made a mental effort to push the doubts aside so he could rest.

From behind him on the train, Klewe could hear the distracting cry of an infant unable to nap. He forced himself to close his eyes and awaited the train's mid-afternoon arrival.

After what seemed only a few more moments, he awakened to the jolt of movement all about him. The train had completed a full stop inside a station. When he saw the sign outside, he recognized it as his destination, so he lifted his umbrella from the train floor.

Outside lay Stratford-upon-Avon, hometown to William Shakespeare. Also, he thought to himself enjoying the coincidence, home to the Teletubbies. The mental image of that television show for very young children brought a fleeting smile to his face as he disembarked, taking an exceedingly long step down from the high train stairs and twisting his ankle slightly when he landed. As he awkwardly crossed the platform, he dodged a small family with their luggage on wheels, before sidestepping an older couple with a rambunctious grandchild in tow. Nobody looked at him or seemed to note his arrival at all. He glanced at his watch and made his way into downtown Stratford toward the main tourist stop on Henley Street.

At the half-timbered building known as Shakespeare's Birthplace, he picked up a map of visitor locations around the historic town. It had been years since his most recent tour, and he did not want to rely on memory to find his way around. In fact, he had not spent much time here since his college days. At that time, he was a graduate student at the University of Virginia, and he took pride in learning that Thomas Jefferson had made this same pilgrimage to Stratford almost 200 years before him. Over those two centuries, though, the small town Jefferson knew had developed at a startling rate.

He unfolded the map and walked slowly along a narrow lane. Suddenly he looked up to find himself face to face with a fiery dragon. It was ensconced in an oversized work of stained glass that took up most of an antique store's front window, depicting Saint George in full battle with the fearsome creature.

The shopkeeper, an elderly man sporting thick eyeglasses, came outside to inspect the walkway. "Lovely piece of glass, isn't it?" he observed, bending arthritically to retrieve somebody's discarded Cadbury wrapper from the walk. "Our beloved George himself."

"Patron saint of England," Klewe said.

"And a killer of dragons," the old man replied in what was undoubtedly part of his sales catechism for potential customers.

Klewe thought for a moment. "Was it somewhere near here that George killed the dragon?"

The store owner seemed caught off-guard. "Heavens, no. But it is a most unusual story. Most people just assume it happened somewhere in this country because he's our patron, but it didn't. George was part of the early Christian church, the evangelical branch that traveled from Rome to places as far away as Africa and

Asia and even came here to England to convert nonbelievers to the faith. Some historians think he fought the dragon in Turkey. But many scholars now place the actual encounter near a lake in northern Africa. In Algeria, they say. Does make you wonder, doesn't it?"

"About what?"

The old man pushed his eyeglasses higher on the bridge of his nose. "If the world hasn't always been smaller than we think. Who else might have already been coming to England in the days of the Roman empire? It would make quite a difference to our world view, don't you think?"

Klewe thanked the man for his time. As he walked on, he recalled his college days, when he meandered through Stratford's streets and pretended he was Shakespeare himself, out for a stroll of his village. Now he began to wonder, though, if England in the old days had really been any more accepting of difference than it was now. He wanted to think so, but he knew better. Klewe thought of "The Tempest" and its telling piece of dialogue that the Londoners of Shakespeare's time would sooner part with their money to see a dead Indian than to help a live beggar. Ruefully he doubted that people had changed very much over the centuries.

That passage from "The Tempest" made him recall the National Archives quotation Zelda had spotted a few days earlier. Shakespeare's words—"What's past is prologue"—began to echo in his mind, propelling him forward faster with each step. No matter what had gone on, he thought, he would need to be ready now. And this time he fought off the shudder he'd felt coming.

Chapter 48.

RAPIDLY BYPASSING ALL the quaint village shops of Stratford, Klewe pressed on, at one point nearing Hall's Croft, the restored house of Shakespeare's older daughter who had married a doctor. Inside that residence was a small tearoom, and his heart pounded faster for an instant when he saw a young blond woman seated inside. It was not Zelda.

He knew that another left turn would have taken him past the main stage of the Royal Shakespeare Company and around to the banks of the Avon River, but he turned right instead to get there faster. A rowdy group of American students, laughing and pointing, passed in front of him. He gazed beyond them, awestruck by a familiar building topped with a graceful spire. It was Stratford's Holy Trinity Church, what he'd told Zelda only a few days ago was his power source.

He forced himself forward, fighting an increasing sense of desolation about what he might find there. Inside the wide doors to the church, he waited beside an entry table where a rotund man with a languid expression sat collecting entrance fees. Although entering the church itself is free, he noted how it cost money to see Shakespeare's gravestone inside. He paid the going rate and looked over the people grouped in small numbers throughout the sanctuary, but without recognizing any of them.

Coming up to the front of Holy Trinity, he glanced to the side of the altar where a painted bust of Shakespeare stared out over the congregational pews. It was a weekday afternoon, so there were many visitors, but no church service in progress. He examined the bust, wondering how it might have looked before the refurbishing that caused it to be repainted. It matched the one on display in the Folger's reading room, and he reflected on the awful events of the last few days. Maybe, he began to wonder, knowing the truth about Shakespeare was meant to be some kind of curse, a truth too dangerous to be revealed.

The thought of a curse moved him toward the main altar. Directly in front of the altar lay the great gray stone atop Shakespeare's tomb, and he bent over to study the epitaph on the stone. A high-pitched voice beside him spoke the words aloud as he silently read them. It was the exhilarated tones of an elderly Irish tourist, a gray-haired woman who bowed almost to the ground while repeating the Bard's last words.

"'Good friend, for Jesus' sake, forbear to dig the dust enclosed here. Blessed be he that spares these stones." She brought her wrinkled hands together as if in prayer. "Glory," she whispered excitedly to Klewe with an inquisitive glance, "do you suppose Shakespeare himself wrote that?"

"No one knows for sure," he said, "but it wouldn't surprise me. You missed a line, though."

"Oh, yes, I see," she said, casting her eyes lower to finish reading the four-line epitaph, "And cursed be he that moves my bones." She stood back up as best she could. "Why, then," she winked a clear blue eye at him, "I must be blessed, because I wouldn't consider moving him anywhere." She started to wander away, then turned back to Klewe. "He surely did write that last part."

"Why do you say that?"

"Well, why else would he call them 'my bones'?" She winked once more and offered a brief smile before she left.

Klewe would have returned the smile, if her words had not struck him so hard. He spun back to the tombstone and crouched to look again at the final line of its quatrain.

"My bones." The final message texted to him by Mason Everly.

Here Klewe stood in the center of N35, reading the words "my bones." They were right there upon the stone, the last of Shakespeare's famous last words. He stood back up, looking silently at the letters as they whirled about in his mind and reformed themselves in various orders. Yes, he slowly realized, Shakespeare must have written them. And now, staring at them, he finally knew why they were so important.

As he straightened himself to his full height, he felt a hand laid gently upon his forearm. He started to turn around, but before he had the chance, the distinct scent of lilacs washed over him. A woman spoke quietly into his ear, and her French accent was unmistakable.

"I expect you'll be wanting to see your wife."

Chapter 49.

WHEELING SWIFTLY ABOUT, Klewe found himself staring once again into the brownish-green eyes of Blanche Corneille. "White Crow," he said at last, his tone uninflected and without emotion.

"So," she smiled with tight-pressed lips, "you have managed to translate my name. I had hoped that might convince you to return home."

"That and your little bomb joke, I suppose?"

"Yes," she said regretfully. "We could get no PE-4 into France." Blanche's pronunciation of the plastic explosive did indeed sound like "pay a cat."

Klewe's eyes wandered the sanctuary before returning to Blanche. "At least I managed to find you."

"Managed to?" Blanche shook her head disdainfully. "We were counting on that. Why else would we allow your wife to leave a message in Westminster Abbey?"

"Where is Zelda?" he demanded. She said nothing, but angled him sharply to face the back of the church. There, in the last pew, he could see a woman sitting alone, her eyes downcast. He roughly shoved past Blanche, elbowing her aside in his eagerness to get to Zelda. The Frenchwoman followed in close proximity, keeping only a step or two behind him all the way to the rear wall of Holy Trinity. Nobody else was seated in the back pews, and there was no indication Zelda was being held there against her will.

"Are you all right?" Klewe collapsed onto the pew beside her. He did not see the bruising until she lifted her face to him. "My God, what have they done to you?"

"It doesn't matter," she said resignedly, twisting the white-gold ring on her finger.

"No, it does not," agreed a deeper voice, as somebody entered the far end of the pew. Klewe looked up to see the peevish expression of Earl Wrist, now standing on the other side of Zelda. The bald scholar grabbed roughly for Zelda's arm and pulled her up from the pew. "Your husband has arrived. It is best we go outside."

The voice implied a weapon, but it was not until Wrist opened his off-white jacket that Klewe saw the protruding hilt beneath. As a group, they rose together from the back pew and slowly made their way out of the Holy Trinity sanctuary. When Klewe turned for a final glance at the Shakespeare bust, sightseers were now blocking his view. Inside the front door, the heavyset collector's attention had been drawn away to new arrivals.

Once the four were outside in the late afternoon air, Wrist prompted Zelda to turn from the main entrance of the church and head across the surrounding cemetery plots. Klewe followed in short order, with Blanche staying slightly back. They passed along a walkway between rows of uneven graves, with the church and all its visitors fading behind them. Beyond the churchyard cemetery was a small forest, and Wrist directed them forcefully toward those trees.

At the edge of the woods, Zelda broke from Wrist's grasp, but the wrenching movement caused her to fall onto her knees. After she struck the ground, her hand closed around something before she attempted to stand. Klewe tried to help her up, but she rebuked his offer. Once she was on her feet, she thrust both hands into the pockets of her tawny windbreaker. "Get away from me," she insisted bitterly. "I might as well have stayed home and written my own obit."

"It'll be okay." His dismal attempt at comforting words made her spin fiercely about to confront him.

"I warned you about Hal Iger."

Klewe did not understand. "He's in on this too?"

"Too?" she asked incredulously and stared furiously at Wrist, who solidified his hold on Zelda's arm.

"I was Hal Iger," he informed Klewe, "when I was in Washington."

"That's how he knew what the killer said to Mason," Zelda explained. "He was the killer, and he's been playing with us ever since."

"When I came back to London," Wrist continued, "I removed my contacts and shaved my head in order to become Earl Wrist." He strong-armed Zelda to move forward. "This one refused to be intimidated by me at Kennedy Center. I keep hoping you two will back off, but you won't leave it alone, will you?"

"Let Zelda go," Klewe urged. "She's not part of this. Just a friend."

"Your friend?" Blanche scoffed. "You mean your wife."

"Neither," Zelda replied sadly.

Klewe tried to divert Wrist's attention by asking him, "Why did you use Raleigh's name?"

"A fitting identity for the School of Night, don't you think? Had you not been so intent on your theory, you might have realized sooner."

Klewe could feel his discomfort mounting as the trees gave way to a clearing near the banks of the Avon. Not far off were the noises of passengers in the small boats weaving among swans on the river. He noticed that Zelda had begun to tremble and asked if she wanted his blazer, but she ignored him.

"Your professor friend back in D.C. was, well, unfortunately far too invested in the story," Wrist continued, fingering a small rectangular object from his shirt pocket. "I couldn't dissuade him at all." Klewe recognized that Wrist held a flash drive, most likely the one containing Mason Everly's research. At the same moment Wrist was reaching inside his waistband to withdraw a long pointed dagger with a familiar Renaissance design.

It was a main-gauche stained with blood.

Chapter 50.

KLEWE NEEDED TIME to think. He could discern no sign of rescue close at hand and tried urging the older man to keep talking. "Tell me about White Crow."

Wrist seemed genuinely surprised by the request. He ordered Zelda harshly forward through straggly brush near the shoreline. "What are you asking me?"

"Who you really are."

"As if that matters either," the older man said dismissively. "We go by various names, White Crow among them, as one group in the School of Night. That organization hardly noticed us at first."

"When was that?"

"Years ago, back when I met Blanche. We married and started a family. But then we lost Lila, our only daughter, in a hit-and-run. Yes, we have those crimes in Europe too. Vehicular homicide, they called it, with reports of a dark-skinned man behind the wheel."

"You saw the driver?" Zelda asked, but Wrist ignored the question. "Or maybe you needed somebody to blame. Maybe an entire race?"

Wrist did not deign to respond to her. Instead, he continued his explanation for Klewe. "That's when we moved to London and formed our splinter cell to assist the parent group with special projects. Blanche and I work well together, don't you think?"

"You'll be arrested for this," Zelda said angrily.

"I don't think so," Blanche answered, inching Zelda closer to the water's edge. Only Klewe stayed mindfully back from the slippery bank. "The authorities will find nothing about us with the names you know."

"And all your research," Wrist said, raising the flash drive above his head, "will be equally hard to find." With a flick of his right hand, he launched the object high above the river. It floated in the air momentarily and then fell into the murky water below. Klewe, unable to move toward the river, felt sickened as it disappeared beneath the surface. Zelda watched him first with expectation and then exasperation. She started toward the water herself, but Blanche blocked the way.

Wrist turned to face Klewe. "I went to Washington hoping to prevent your colleague from making his talk this evening. But he refused to be discouraged from that goal. After he died, I had to inject myself into the investigation to mislead the police. And then there was all the trouble with that woman outside the cabin." Klewe's fury flared at this blunt dismissal of Amanda Everly as nothing more than an obstacle in White Crow's path. "Not to mention the Vespa and Cadillac you cost me. And then there was Paris."

"I only went there," Klewe interrupted, wiping an increasingly sweaty palm against his pants leg, "because of Mason's itinerary."

"We had tried to lure him there unsuccessfully," Blanche observed, "but our French campus served us well in distracting the two of you." She smiled wryly at Zelda. "Until I saw that young man sitting with you at the café."

"Pierre Camion. What had he ever done to you?"

"Nothing, but I could tell he was helping you. That was something we could not allow."

Klewe was dumbfounded. "All he did was translate your name for us. What were you thinking?"

"And what would Lila think?" Zelda asked.

Blanche walked over to Zelda and slapped her hard across the face, then struggled to regain an attitude of detachment. "Isn't it shameful," she said indifferently, "how some Europeans insist on attaching themselves to visiting Americans?"

Wrist picked up the thread of the story. "And still you wouldn't go away. When you came to Southwark, I thought about taking care of you there. But you had your guard with you, so I tried warning you off one last time. You don't listen well, my dear friend. That's why we knew you'd rush to Stratford to rescue her."

"Some rescue," Zelda said flatly.

"You must know you're going to fail," Klewe told him. "Even without my talk tonight, the media will get hold of the story and run with it."

"Perhaps they will," the older man said. "But which do you honestly believe will make the more sensational news story—a dry lesson in literary history or a series of international murders? And, by the way, exactly how did you two rate a guard in London?"

"You can thank Detective Edmund Robinson for that."

"A detective named Edmund?" He gave a dry laugh. "Too bad you talked to the wrong bastard. But there's no reason for us to worry. In our line of work, we've learned that controlling how a story is told can be almost as good as suppressing it altogether."

Zelda balked at his words. "All of this just to make sure Shakespeare remains a Dead White Male?"

"Well," Wrist reminded her, "we all make his praise." He extended the dagger toward Zelda first. Klewe did not watch for her response. He had glanced upstream to where Wallie Chambers was positioning herself along the shore, angling for a clear shot.

"I'm sorry, Zelda," Klewe told her earnestly. "I didn't mean for any of this to happen." She blinked her eyes at him, but said nothing. As Blanche held tightly to Zelda's arms, Wrist brought the dagger around hard.

Klewe lunged between Zelda and the blade. The sharp point drove into his right shoulder, its pain dropping him to one knee. Wrist stumbled backward a step and lifted the blade again. With a sweeping motion, Zelda pulled her hand free from her jacket pocket and raised her closed fist to the older man's neck. There she loosened her grip, dropping a handful of dirt within his shirt collar.

"What the hell?" Wrist gasped, trying to shake whatever it was off him.

"Spiders," Zelda answered with a sardonic grin, the first time Klewe had seen her smile since he got to Stratford.

Wrist tugged at his buttoned shirt, letting the dagger slip from his fingers. Klewe, still kneeling, drove his body forward into Wrist's legs, and the two men fell sideways together into the slow-moving waters of the Avon River.

Chapter 51.

STILL STANDING ON the bank, Blanche felt the sharp-
ness of Zelda's elbow digging into her side. The two had rushed at
each other once the men fell into the river. Zelda, her eyes pinned
to the sharp weapon on the ground, pushed off from the older
woman and grabbed the fallen dagger.

Water splashed everywhere from the submerged struggle of
the two men flailing to breathe while jockeying for position. They
alternated coming up long enough to gasp for air and continue
their battle. When Wrist wrestled him down again, Klewe suddenly
felt terror at the realization of being under the surface of the river.

Anxiously they pushed against each other, trying to leverage
themselves above the water line. For what seemed like an endless
moment of combat, they traded turns surfacing into the brisk au-
tumn air. Finally Klewe placed both hands on Wrist and pushed
him down hard by the shoulders, simultaneously lifting himself
above water. He could tell the fight was over as the other man's
body drifted away from him in the current.

Choking loudly, Klewe then hoisted himself out of the water
in time to hear a gunshot from upstream. He tried to snatch at
Wrist, but the older man disappeared beneath the surface. Klewe
jerked himself back around to check for Wallie's arrival on the

shore. Blanche stood submissively behind Zelda, who held the dagger now to the woman's throat.

"Your ring is gone, Madame," Blanche observed coldly.

"Mademoiselle," Zelda corrected her, barely glancing at the empty spot on her finger. "And I don't need that ring anymore."

Wallie knelt down where Klewe had collapsed onto the dry ground. He lay there inhaling loudly while she tended to his bleeding shoulder. A long moment of silence was finally broken when Blanche spoke again.

"Where's Earl?" she insisted apprehensively. All eyes turned to the water, but Wrist had never resurfaced.

Wallie turned to Zelda and asked, "Are you all right?" The reporter nodded quietly, still holding the dagger while Klewe was being helped to his feet. He could hear Blanche's voice lashing out at Zelda.

"Do you realize what you have done?"

"I'm sorry you lost your daughter," Zelda began, but Blanche stopped her.

"This is not about Lila. You have come here to desecrate the memory of a great writer. Think what you are saying about Shakespeare. Soon this will be over, and you must know how it will all end."

"What do you mean?"

"It doesn't matter. I have failed, and failure was not an option. I have nothing more to say."

Before the others realized the import of the woman's last words, Blanche had grasped Zelda's hand with the upturned dagger to plunge the weapon into her own neck. As Wallie rushed to stop her, blood spurted everywhere, and Blanche dropped slowly forward out of Zelda's grasp.

Chapter 52.

INSIDE THE TERRACED pub entrance for the Dirty Duck, Wallie Chambers listened raptly to the caller on her cell phone before switching it off. "Blanche didn't make it," she reported to Klewe as they waited for a table. "They tell me she died on the way to the hospital." Her eyes scanned the riverside, once again bustling with swans. "Filthy birds," she muttered before being seated.

"They're not so bad." The tempting aroma of shepherd's pie filled the pub, making Klewe realize how hungry he was. "Did you know they mate for life? Most people aren't that loyal." He peered through the crowd until he spotted Zelda, slowly making her way to their table. When he tried to hold her chair, she gently pushed him down.

"Don't start that chivalry stuff now," she chided him, but then kissed him softly on the cheek. "How do I look?"

"You're beautiful."

"Amazing what a little makeup can do. Where's my vanilla vodka? And what are we discussing?"

"Swans," Wallie told her as the waitress brought the first round.

"A lot of theaters use them in their names," Klewe was saying, "from Oregon to Australia. What fascinated me, though, was learning the black swan was not from England. Here it was long thought to be a mistake of nature or, as a recent book of that name called it, an anomaly. When the British began to colonize Australia, though, they found black swans were native there. It's even the name for an Australian winery. The Black Swan Merlot," he winked at Zelda, "is especially memorable."

"I'll drink to that," Zelda said, signaling for another vanilla vodka from the overworked waitress. She placed a hand onto Klewe's blazer and could tell by his instant reaction how much his shoulder still ached. "You sure you're okay?"

"Sure. Well, my shoes are still soaked through. How's the power tie?" He stretched out his yellow necktie for her approval.

"You'll do. Although I'd rather you had on that white bathrobe I wore at the cabin."

Quickly changing the subject, he lifted his pint of ale to Wallie. "To Special Agent Chambers, whom I owe a big apology for deserting her in Marylebone," he began, but she quickly stopped his toast, taking the drink away from him.

"You'd better not have that," Wallie advised, setting the pint back on the table, "if you want to be sharp for tonight's lecture."

Klewe stared at her in amazement. "What are you talking about? I've missed that by a long shot, haven't I?"

Wallie checked her watch. "Not with a police escort to get there, you haven't. But we have to leave now."

Klewe turned to Zelda. "What do you think?"

"I suppose I could go," she said lightly, "as long as you're not driving."

"Not a chance," Wallie responded, buttoning her trenchcoat to leave.

Klewe glared at the both of them. "Thanks. I'll just finish drying myself off in the back seat."

They climbed in the open doors of a police van and headed for the M1 freeway toward London. Klewe did not bother to clock their speed, but the officer at the wheel was passing every vehicle near them. Wallie rode shotgun, and she squirmed about in her seat to address Klewe and Zelda behind her.

"They haven't found Earl Wrist's body yet. I'm sorry to say the flash drive is gone too."

"I can think of worse outcomes," Klewe responded, and Zelda nodded in solemn agreement. "Wonder if we'll ever find out who Earl and Blanche really were."

"Whatever else you might say," Zelda acknowledged, "Blanche loved her daughter. And she had to be fiercely committed to her cause to stab herself like that."

"Was it really a cause," Wallie wondered, "or just an obsession?"

"Obsession, I'd say," Klewe said, leaning closer to enjoy Zelda's perfume again. "Shakespeare was the ultimate Dead White Male to her. That's what made him a prize worth the risks."

"Maybe so," Zelda replied doubtfully. "But I happen to like the idea of a biracial Shakespeare. And maybe a multicultural approach will make Shakespeare even more popular, somebody who can be shared by everyone." She watched as Klewe's smile faded from his face. "You're thinking about Mason?"

"He'd figured out more of the puzzle. That's what he meant by 'my bones.'"

"What?"

"The epitaph on Shakespeare's gravestone. I realized in Holy Trinity Church that the last two words form an anagram. 'My bones' is an exact joining of the letters in 'Ebony' with 'M.S.,' the initials of Shakespeare's mother."

Zelda looked puzzled. "Was he saying his mother was black?"

"No, I think Shakespeare was being perfectly literal. In his case, 'my bones' would have come from a white mother and a black father, with their biracial union forming the bones of the world's greatest writer. And now, almost 400 years later, the Bard's wordplay gets the last laugh." As they sped toward London, Klewe had started jotting down a brief outline for his talk and then pocketed the notes confidently. "Guess I'm ready with the story."

"Well, maybe you can get away with that," Zelda said. "But I need time to work. In fact, I did as you suggested and called the chief of the Washington bureau from the Dirty Duck. I've already filed my lead."

"Your lead?"

She grabbed his arm excitedly. "The editors are talking a by-line and maybe the front page."

"No more obituary updates for you."

"Not if I can help it." She frowned thoughtfully. "But what do you plan to say in your lecture? I mean, about the last few days?"

"As little as possible. This talk isn't about us or what we've been through. It isn't even about Mason or the others. It's about a secret that needs to come out."

"Secrets always do come out," Wallie chimed in from the front seat. "And you won't need to worry about security tonight. They've conducted a sweep of the room where you'll be speaking, and everything's a go."

They crossed into Southwark and admired the exterior of the resplendent Globe framed in the twilight. Klewe felt Zelda take his hand and squeeze it.

"What was that for?"

"Luck."

He returned the squeeze before turning to Wallie. "Have you spoken with your detective friend in Washington?"

"Briefly, but if I know Edmund, he's going to want every last detail." The police van stopped near a side entrance to the Globe, and Wallie hopped out along with the driver, signaling them to stay seated in the back. After a few minutes, there came a sharp tap at the window, and they also left the van. An unmarked door on the Globe was pushed wide from the inside, and a uniformed officer beckoned for them to enter.

"Wallie?" Klewe called, summoning her away from a security team. "You told me you talked with Edmund?"

"To fill him in."

"I've been thinking about what Wrist said. When I mentioned Edmund, he kind of chuckled and said I'd talked to the wrong bastard."

"Don't know why. So far as I know, the two didn't even know each other. But Eddie will be disappointed no one was brought to justice for this whole mess."

Klewe fell silent a moment. "You're right. So far anyway." He clicked open his Cartier watch and was pleased to find it still running. "Let's call George Taliaferro at the National Portrait Gallery. Maybe we can remedy that."

A short while later, Klewe and Zelda found themselves being paraded into a tightly packed lecture hall. Zelda moved to take a seat at the rear, but Wallie guided her instead to an empty chair in the front row. Klewe waited to be introduced as the night's speaker before taking his place at the lectern.

"None of my previous lectures about Shakespeare," he began, stepping backward from the metallic echo of the microphone, "have had dedications. Tonight's talk, however, is dedicated to my late mentor, Professor Mason Everly. Credit also goes to Amanda Everly and Pierre Camion, two friends without whom this evening," he said, studying the first row of the audience, where Zelda's eyes sparkled in approval, "would not have been possible."

He reached for his scribbled notes, then decided against using them. Gazing steadily out at his audience, he silently surveyed the room filled with scholars and journalists as if looking to solve a great mystery.

"What kind of secret," Klewe asked the assembled Globe listeners to consider, "is worth dying for?"

Chapter 53.

"AND NOW," KLEWE concluded an hour later, "I want to leave all of you with another question, one that my deceased colleague, Mason Everly, posed at the start of our work together. Does it matter, Mason asked me, what Shakespeare's racial identity was? What we sadly realized is that, at least in our time, it does. But it shouldn't. Someday, and we hope that day comes very soon, it no longer will."

Several minutes of applause and animated questions followed, until Klewe was finally escorted from the stage. He was led into a reception area where wine and cheese were to be served to the attendees. There he found a small group waiting to congratulate him on the successful evening.

"Splendid talk, Professor." Jennifer Bristol put out her hand to Klewe, whose shoulder made him wince slightly as he took it. With Wallie and Zelda at his side, he smiled at George Taliaferro's assistant. "Sorry we arrived late, but so did your invitation. I'm sure Mr. Taliaferro will be quite upset he couldn't attend."

"Yes, Professor, it really is a most exciting and original premise." The publisher Ed Allenby, standing behind her, extended his hand as well. "I'm glad Jennifer insisted I come with her."

"I can already picture the cover of Time," Zelda told them enthusiastically.

"The publicity should be truly amazing," Allenby agreed.

"As you were counting on, I'm sure," Klewe told him, turning back to Jennifer. "Did you look in his desk as I asked?"

The young woman nodded ringlets of red hair. "Here it is," she said, producing a handkerchief-wrapped object from her purse. She delicately uncovered a letter opener and handed it to Klewe.

"What's going on here?" Allenby objected. "That's personal property. She's taken it from my office."

"Yes, at my request. I thought I recognized the emblem engraved in the handle."

"My family crest," Allenby said, unsuccessfully trying to wrestle the opener from Klewe's fist, "but I fail to see what business it is of yours."

Jennifer looked innocently at him. "The Gloucester family crest, isn't it?" The surprised publisher nodded.

Klewe tapped the letter opener against his palm. "It was Earl Wrist who gave you away. When I mentioned to him a detective named Edmund, he made a joke that I'd talked with the wrong bastard. I wasn't thinking of 'King Lear' at the time, but the most famous bastard in all of Shakespeare appears in that play, and his name happens to be Edmund."

"So?" Zelda asked.

"So Mr. Allenby here is named Ed, which is usually short for Edward or Edgar. In his office the other day, though, there was a photo on the roll-top desk. He told us it was a picture of his namesake, the Hillary who climbed Everest, whose first name was—"

"Edmund," Jennifer completed the sentence, narrowing her eyes in the direction of the publisher.

"That's true." Allenby glared impudently at Klewe.

"But what does that have to do," Zelda wondered, "with the family crest on his letter opener?"

"It's the Lear connection," Jennifer explained. "Edmund's father in the play is the Earl of Gloucester."

"Exactly right," Klewe asserted, and all eyes turned to the publisher.

Ed Allenby stepped back a pace and took a deep breath. "So what if I knew Wrist? And, yes, I did talk with your friend Everly. I made him a most generous offer to publish your book when it's ready. I think he would have talked you into accepting, had he lived, so I certainly had nothing to do with his death."

"But you did have something to gain," Klewe said, "both you and White Crow."

"A book on Shakespeare is always bankable," Allenby admitted, speaking candidly for the first time. "But consider the possibilities with this book and the School of Night. What if your theory sparked rumors of an international conspiracy, fueled by racism and even murder? Now you're talking not just a best-seller, but a mega-seller. I had to take the chance."

Zelda gave him a disdainful look. "So you were the money behind White Crow?"

He stared at her unapologetically. "I value Shakespeare, and I hate seeing him dismissed these days as one more Dead White Male. Your vision of him as the Ebony Swan could change all that. And what's more, the cell known as White Crow would be publicizing the book with every move they made. People have been known to kill for that kind of publicity." When he realized how true his final words were, Allenby fell silent.

Wallie looked at Klewe. "How deeply do you think he was involved with the School of Night and especially White Crow?"

"All we'll have to do is follow the money," Zelda said.

"Your next big story," Klewe suggested.

Allenby began to cough deeply, then uncontrollably, nearly doubling over. Casually he slid his left hand into his coat pocket.

From behind him, Wallie's resonant voice responded with a preemptive suggestion.

"Don't try it," she warned him. She watched as Allenby extracted only a folded handkerchief from his pocket and coughed again. Using his right hand, he shoved Zelda roughly into Klewe, knocking them both off balance while he tried to get away. With an agile leap, Special Agent Chambers shouldered the publisher onto the hard floor, landing awkwardly on top of him. As members of the Globe's security staff pulled Allenby back to his feet, Wallie remained sprawled on the ground. As she attempted to rise, her face was contorted with pain.

"Are you all right?" Klewe knelt next to her.

"It's this damned ankle," she said, unable to stand. "I think I broke it. Tell me, Professor, why do I always wind up injured around you?"

"I don't know," he answered her softly, "but that was one impressive tackle."

Wallie forced a pained smile. "Real fans never forget football."

As Allenby was led away, he cast a satisfied glance at Klewe. "More grist for the publicity mill," he asserted before being escorted from the hall.

Klewe made a disgusted face. "He's right, you know. He won't get punished for what White Crow did, even if he bankrolled them. And he'll probably wind up selling more of his books." He waited until medical assistance had arrived for Wallie, then headed quickly toward the Globe's front doors. Zelda followed in close pursuit.

Outside the theater, they hurried along the darkened streets of Southwark. In silence they passed beside Rose Tower and came upon an alley with the warehouse Klewe had seen before. As they approached the desolate building, he slowed and gestured for Zelda to stay behind him. Unwilling to remain in the background, she pushed past him to try the door. It was unlocked.

"Is someone here?" Zelda called, peering into the building before flicking on a switch inside the entrance. A weak beam of yellow light washed the bleak walls of the warehouse, showing little more than a desk and a wall clock. "What is this place?" She moved forward to see several closed doors along a carpeted hallway.

"Careful," Klewe cautioned her. "Remember what happened in Paris."

"Yeah, right," she responded. "That poor guy must still be looking for his groceries." Her hands settled on the back of a roll-away chair behind the desk. "I also remember your test for explosives."

Before Klewe could stop her, Zelda grasped the top of the chair solidly and, with great effort, managed to heave the chair down the hall. She was able to send it reeling partway along the corridor until its wheels stopped abruptly on the Berber carpet.

"See?" she told Klewe. "Nothing."

It was then they heard a door at the distant end of the hall being opened. When she squinted her eyes, she could barely make out a figure in the pitch-dark doorway, but she sensed instantly that the man in the shadows was Earl Wrist.

Chapter 54.

BEFORE KLEWE OR Zelda could say anything, the bald man lumbered down the hallway toward them. Dressed in a fresh off-white suit, Earl Wrist seemed to be having difficulty walking. He stopped and, with a copious sweep of his arm, invited them to come closer.

"Welcome back," Wrist officiously announced to Klewe , "to the School of Night." He pushed his thick-lensed glasses back against his face, but the visitors came no closer. "You'll need to pay attention. What was it Shakespeare said?" Wrist tugged tauntingly at his own ear lobe and mimed cutting it off. "'Lend me your ears.'" He grinned cruelly at them.

Klewe felt rage boiling up inside him. Zelda looked about for a weapon, but nothing useful was nearby. Klewe moved stealthily forward to interpose himself between the two of them. As Wrist laughed coarsely, they could see an open bottle of Dewar's dangling from his left hand.

"Ever the protector," Wrist noted to Klewe. "Too bad you could not save your friends. And my Blanche as well." He sounded more circumspect than sorrowful. "She was a rare beauty in an ugly world."

"A white crow?" Zelda suggested.

"I won't live to see another." He took a tentative step toward them. "And our poor Lila too. I wasn't watching when she ran into the street. Her death was my fault, you know, but I could never bring myself to tell Blanche . Perhaps she knows now. If so, she also knows how sorry I am."

The unrepentant expression on the scholar's face bothered Klewe, prompting him to change the subject. "We passed by the Rose Theater again. Did you know 'Titus Andronicus' was first staged there? Shakespeare himself may have played Aaron the Moor."

The older man gave a twisted smile and waved the Scotch bottle at him. "So you've revealed Shakespeare's secret to the world. We knew it was coming. Your friend Everly caught our attention when he asked about Sonnet 55 on the Internet. You've studied, I presume, the references to Shakespeare by his contemporaries?"

"Yes, we have."

"All of them?" Wrist scoffed softly, almost to himself. "People claim nobody in Shakespeare's time noticed his existence, but there were lots of comments about him and his writings. Of course, as you know, only a handful mentioned his physical appearance."

"Three, to be exact."

"Did you include Ben Jonson's words in that total?" Klewe shook his head slightly. "Then you've left out the most important witness against your theory, Shakespeare's closest friend and rival playwright. You cannot ignore what Jonson said about Shakespeare in the First Folio."

"That wasn't printed until seven years after Shakespeare's death."

"Ben Jonson would not have forgotten what his friend looked like, and what does he tell us? That the Folio's engraver 'hath hit his face.' There's absolutely no doubt in that statement and no reference to race at all."

"But Jonson also says, 'Reader, look not on his picture, but his book.' As if the picture didn't do Shakespeare justice."

"What's your point?"

"Ben Jonson needed to keep the truth quiet. He was smart enough to know that Shakespeare's words would live on, and he must have known how history would judge his own work in comparison. Did Jonson really want history asserting that a biracial man was capable of outwriting him? I don't think so."

When Klewe paused to catch his breath, Wrist blurted out, "But aren't you assuming Jonson was a racist?"

"You bet I am. As racist as the whole School of Night. And Jonson himself left very little room for doubt about it. Have you ever read his 'Masque of Blackness'?"

"What about it?"

"While Shakespeare was busy enriching the world with 'Othello,' Ben Jonson wrote a masque about black women who come from Africa to visit London. When they go swimming in the Thames, they're suddenly made beautiful. And how does that happen? According to Jonson, the English river washes away their blackness, and they're turned white. Doesn't that sound racist to you?"

Wrist stayed silent a long while, shaking his head.

"Don't you get it?" Klewe asked. "Jonson's masque proves there was racism in Shakespeare's day. People have this wrongheaded notion that there were no blacks in England back then, an idea that's patently false. Of course, denying the truth helped racism to flourish and allowed a School of Night conspiracy."

"Or perhaps you have invented a conspiracy theory just for the sake of being controversial."

"Hell, if that were true, I wouldn't just be suggesting that the Bard was biracial. I'd be asking whether Robert Greene acted alone, or had he been coerced way back when into insulting Shakespeare in print? In other words, if there was a conspiracy, did your School of Night use a dying man to do their dirty work for them? At least I haven't gone there."

"Not yet." Wrist closed his eyes wearily, and Klewe could tell something was terribly off in the older man's demeanor. He waved Zelda to move behind him toward the front door.

"You're wrong," Wrist said simply, opening his eyes. "About all of it."

"You refuse to accept that Shakespeare was biracial, even though it gave him his power. Shakespeare knew that it's multiculturalism that makes us better and stronger human beings. People thrive on variety, not sameness, and Shakespeare knew better than anybody, because he'd actually lived it, the outsider on the inside. Remember the way he extolled Cleopatra's greatness? He wrote, 'Age cannot wither her, nor custom stale her infinite variety.'"

Klewe could hear Zelda opening the outside door, but he was trying desperately to remember something Blanche said about not being able to get PE-4 into France. His eyes feverishly searched the hallway in front of Wrist and finally spotted the thin piece of wire stretched slightly above floor level.

The older man pointed his open bottle at Klewe. "The School of Night ordered White Crow to discredit you," Wrist said tiredly. "Perhaps we have failed at that, but I still wonder whether you believe what you're saying. Are you really convinced?"

It was the question Klewe had long tried to evade, but he no longer felt reluctant to answer. "I used to be skeptical," he said and then smiled. "Now I'm sure of it."

Wrist stared at him a moment and then deliberately tumbled forward, falling onto the trip wire. It pulled itself tight, setting off an initial explosion inside the long hallway. While Klewe and Zelda sped from the warehouse, they heard a second explosion being triggered, and then a third, in a series of detonations that billowed through the far reaches of the School of Night.

Chapter 55.

Washington, D.C., early November

CHRISTOPHER KLEWE PACED eagerly inside the tall front doors of Kennedy Center and pushed up the sleeves of his multicolored sweater. He saw Zelda arriving outside and stood stockstill as she approached him. She brushed back strands of blond hair from the London sweatshirt she was wearing, and they shared a lingering hug. It had been barely a week since they met.

"Almost didn't recognize you," Zelda teased, "without the umbrella." She gave him a big smile and excitedly dug down into her shoulder bag. "I have something for you if I can find it." At last she pulled out a fresh pack of Wrigley's.

Klewe reached for the gum. "I'm touched."

"That's mine," she reprimanded him playfully. Then she placed a weathered leatherbound volume into his hands. "I spent the morning combing through old bookstores in Georgetown for this. Figured your copy got ruined in the water."

"A collection of Shakespeare's sonnets?" He paged through the book carefully, appreciating the gold-tooled binding in dark crimson morocco. "Thank you. That was really thoughtful."

"Now you can explain them all to me."

He turned to the conclusion of Sonnet 55 and read aloud, "'You live in this, and dwell in lovers' eyes.'" He kissed her, and they locked arms to walk the plush red carpeting into the Grand Foyer. Once again inside that enormous room, they were greeted immediately by the stern appearance of Detective Robinson, swooping down on them in a black suit.

"Paris?" he bellowed gruffly. "Paris? That's your idea of not going far?" His face mellowed, and he shook hands with them both. "Sounds like you had an eventful trip."

"You can ask Wallie all about it," Zelda told him. "By the way, her ankle is healing nicely."

"I already talked with her, and she said to thank you again for that football scarf. I'm really glad you two could meet me here today. Even if you don't listen well." They each gave him a guilty glance before attempting to explain, but the detective shrugged it off. "I know, I know. Not your fault. Well, White Crow is out of business, if not the entire School of Night. At least they'll be slowed down looking for new headquarters."

"Did they find anybody else in the building with him?" Klewe asked.

"No other remains, but they're still investigating. No word yet from Interpol on the real identities of Earl and Blanche."

Zelda looked glum. "And no flash drive?"

The detective shook his head. "Come over here. There's somebody I want you to meet." He walked them to the Opera House steps, where a teenage boy in gray sweats was waiting impatiently. "My son Kenneth," he introduced the lanky student, who shifted uncomfortably from one foot to the other.

"Is this the guy?" Kenneth asked, looking almost suspiciously at Klewe until his father nodded. Then he put out his hand.

"Hi, Kenneth," Klewe said, shaking hands with him. "Your father tells me you're a big fan of poetry."

"Or the girls in English class," Detective Robinson said.

"Dad!" Kenneth whined in exaggerated embarrassment, turning the short word into several syllables.

"'So long as men can breathe,'" Klewe prompted him, "'or eyes can see ...'"

Kenneth gave him a big grin and concluded, "'So long lives this, and this gives life to thee.'" The words spilled sweetly across the red-carpeted foyer and captured the attention of tourists standing by the bronze Kennedy sculpture. Klewe noticed once again how the President's giant face seemed to gaze directly across the large hall and into the Opera House.

"Well done," Klewe told Kenneth. "I hope you'll be considering William and Mary in a few years."

On the Millennium Stage at the far end of the Grand Foyer, a dozen Jamaican students were being lined up on a series of risers. Soon the children's chorus began to flood the open space with a reggae take on "Greensleeves," unlike any version of the song Klewe had ever heard.

He turned to the detective and asked, "So that publisher Allenby wasn't with White Crow? Just paying their way?"

"To help sell a book not even published yet. An evil plan but brilliant," Robinson admitted begrudgingly.

"Well, I'm not willing to give him credit," Klewe replied. "I'm not that forgiving."

Zelda sighed. "Me neither. Do you think Shakespeare was?"

"Maybe." Klewe considered. "You remember how Robert Greene called him an 'upstart crow'? Years after the man died, Shakespeare decided to adapt a story written by Greene into his play 'The Winter's Tale,' so I guess he'd forgiven him by then."

Before moving closer to the children's choir down the hallway, Detective Robinson and his son exchanged goodbyes with them. When Klewe tried pointing Zelda toward the terrace doors, she looked at him questioningly. "But the river's out there."

"I know."

"And I know from Wallie that you ran across Millennium Bridge to find me." Zelda stared directly at him, her eyes beginning to well. "Your brother would have been proud of you. Mason would be too. And I know I am." She cupped his face in her hands and kissed him. "Doesn't it seem like forever since we were here trying to figure out N35?"

"I've been mulling that over," he said. "You know, Mason always did like ambiguity. The way things can have more than one meaning at the same time."

"So?" She watched with curiosity as Klewe went bounding up the short steps into the empty Opera House. A moment afterward, he emerged, triumphantly holding a small rectangular object over his head.

"The flash drive?" Zelda asked, stunned. "Where was it?"

"N35, exactly where Mason said. Orchestra row N, wedged in between Seats 3 and 5."

While the student rendition of "Greensleeves" continued to fill Kennedy Center, several listeners along the Grand Foyer had spontaneously started dancing to the lively Renaissance tune. A celebratory Klewe held out his arms for Zelda to join him.

"But you can't dance," she objected vehemently. "That's what you said. Can you imagine anybody lying like that?"

"Never."

"I do love this song, though." She started to embrace him, then stopped short. "Please don't tell me Shakespeare wrote it."

"Of course not. It's by Henry the Eighth." He looked deeply into her eyes. "But think this through. Shakespeare ends tragedies with death and comedies with dance. He makes us consider the best way to live. That's the most important question there is." She noticed his hands tremble slightly. His face grew serious, and he tried not to sound portentous. "Which reminds me. There's something I have to tell you."

Placing an index finger to his mouth, Zelda crinkled her nose and stepped forward into Klewe's arms.

"Think this through," she whispered into his ear. "Shut up and dance."

Southwark, United Kingdom, later that day

The woman stood carefully within the shadows of the warehouse district, watching the clean-up crews hard at work. She rubbed at the uncomfortable bandage across her throat and tried nibbling at a bear claw she'd bought that morning from a London bakery.

At twilight she remained watching until the final worker departed for the day. Then she took a white-gold ring from her pocket and, pausing to admire its dull luster, pushed it squarely onto her finger. The headlights of a passing car caused her eyes to flash hazel, before she disappeared without a sound down Rose Alley.

Night was almost here.

Epilogue

Southwark, England, late October 1594

AT A BOARDING house not far from the Rose, the lanky youth stood trembling inside a sparsely furnished room. The room's tenant, himself a new player in London, tried to coax the boy for details of what he had witnessed.

"I don't know, sir," the youth kept saying. "I can't rightly tell you what happened there. They would not let me in to see, but afterward I did find this." With a flourish, he produced a neatly folded handkerchief from the pouch he wore at his waist, and he began unfolding the edges to unwrap something. "A lump of his ear, it is," the boy offered as the player carefully fingered the delicate mass. "And I did hear them say, sir, that a player is to be next. A player!"

His emphasis of the last word included an upturned palm. Once the tenant delivered a fistful of coins into his palm, the boy turned hurriedly and fled the room, banging its door closed behind him.

The player nervously rolled the small piece of flesh between his thumb and forefinger. He had already spent sleepless nights considering what response he should make to a group that so despised him, a group that thrived on its anonymity. Now, he reasoned as he moved to the writing table, the decision had been made for him.

With a firm dark hand, he lifted a quill from beside an inkwell and flattened the page before him. He read carefully until he came to the passage where his writing had tentatively stopped. This time, however, the words began to flow freely, words that could mean for him the difference between life and death.

First, he designated the speaker of the new speech to be the King of Navarre. Then he paused to weigh the words the King was about to deliver.

"'O paradox!'" the young player wrote, his hand no longer shaking. "'Black is the badge of hell, the hue of dungeons and the school of night.'" He tapped the quill gently against the table. "The school of night," he read over to himself, satisfied with the wording. Whatever might happen now, at least the world would know he'd had the courage to identify his adversaries in print. The player slowly put down his pen and sighed deeply.

The world would know.

The End

Author's Note

ONLY ONCE DOES the infamous School of Night get mentioned in the writings of William Shakespeare. This hapax legomenon, as the Greeks called a single occurrence of a term throughout a writer's canon, appears in the penultimate act of "Love's Labor's Lost." In that comedy, probably written in the 1590's, the King of Navarre observes:

> O paradox! Black is the badge of hell,
> The hue of dungeons and the school of night.

That passage is frequently cited by Shakespearean scholars as a reference to Sir Walter Raleigh's clandestine gathering of Elizabethan intellectuals and artists, also referred to as the School of Atheism. Raleigh's secret society has been one of the enduring mysteries of Renaissance England, spawning a series of questions ranging from its membership to its mission. In fact, no one can say to this day whether the mysterious School of Night exists.

For the most part, however, the locations in the novel do exist, from the little-known "bird room" of Washington's Kennedy Center to the Globe Theater's bookshop in London and even the pub in Stratford-upon-Avon called the Dirty Duck.

In addition, all of Shakespeare's works and those of his contemporaries referred to throughout the novel are accurately quoted (mostly with modernized spelling, capitalization and punctuation) and are widely available in print. It was Shakespeare's contemporary Robert Greene, for instance, who first called the Stratford playwright an "upstart crow" in a posthumous 1592 pamphlet. Ben Jonson, another of Shakespeare's colleagues, identified the Bard in the First Folio of 1623 as the "Sweet Swan of Avon."

Finally, the first letters of the lines in Sonnet 55 indisputably do contain an anagram of the words "Ebony Swan." It is a most intriguing clue to Shakespeare's secret, a secret that would certainly help explain how the Bard infused ordinary words with such extraordinary wisdom. That wisdom was described most eloquently by Ralph Waldo Emerson, who once said, "Shakespeare taught us that the little world of the heart is vaster, deeper and richer than the spaces of astronomy."

About the Author

Jeffrey Hunter McQuain, who lives in Maryland, holds a Ph. D. in Literary Studies from American University. For more than a dozen years, he served as the researcher for William Safire's "On Language" column in The New York Times. Co-author of the popular books "Coined by Shakespeare" and "The Bard on the Brain," he has extensively taught and occasionally performed in the Bard's plays. "The Shakespeare Conspiracy," his first novel, is based on his nonfiction book "Ebony Swan: The Case for Shakespeare's Race." Go to www.btglobe.com for more information.

CPSIA information can be obtained at www.ICGtesting.com
Printed in the USA
LVOW12s2254010615

440724LV00001B/208/P